D1108318

J Smith
Smith, Sherwood
Trouble under Oz

$17.89
ocm70803263
1st ed.   05/04/2007

Trouble Under Oz

Trouble Under Oz

SHERWOOD SMITH

Illustrated by WILLIAM STOUT

Authorized by the Estate of L. FRANK BAUM

A BYRON PREISS BOOK
HarperCollins*Publishers*

TROUBLE UNDER OZ

A Byron Preiss Book

Text copyright © 2006 by The Baum Trust
and Byron Preiss Visual Publications, Inc.

Jacket and interior illustrations copyright © 2006 by William Stout

Book design by Abbate Design

Library of Congress Cataloging-in-Publication Data is available.

ISBN-10: 0-06-029609-7 — ISBN-13: 978-0-06-029609-4
ISBN-10: 0-06-029610-0 (lib. bdg.) — ISBN-13: 978-0-06-029610-0 (lib. bdg.)

1 2 3 4 5 6 7 8 9 10

FIRST EDITION

To Byron Preiss,

whose vision, energy, and joy in the magic and

possibility of all forms of Story made him the

Great Wizard of New York. He will be missed,

but his work lives on.

ACKNOWLEDGMENTS

First and foremost, thanks to David Hulan, author of *The Glass Cat of Oz*, who generously vetted not only the story, but my Oz details, so that I would get them right. (Any mistakes are my own, not his.) To Howard Zimmerman at Byron Preiss Visual Publications, who worked with me on my initial drafts, and to Melanie Donovan at HarperCollins, whose faith and vision in the project have been significantly responsible for this book seeing the light of day. And to William Stout, whose exquisite illustrations evoke the magic of Oz.

Trouble Under Oz

GUSTS OF ICY WIND
chased across the Kansas landscape and moaned under the
eaves of a little clapboard house halfway along an ordinary
street on the outskirts of Lawrence. Cozy golden light
glowed in the twin attic windows of that house, each window belonging to a small bedroom.

Emma sat in the left-hand room. Her feet curled around
the rungs of her chair as she concentrated on a round glass
snow globe she held in her hands. It was an old snow globe,
its wooden base marred a little by tooth marks that looked
as if they had been made by a small dog.

The snow globe had been passed along from cousins to
nieces and finally to Emma's grandmother. She had given it
to Emma and her sister, Dori, with the story that it had
once belonged to Dorothy Gale.

Yes, *that* Dorothy Gale.

The Dorothy who had been carried to Oz on a cyclone, and who, after many adventures, had finally moved permanently to Oz, along with her dog, Toto, and her Uncle Henry and Aunt Em.

Before last summer Emma hadn't believed that there ever was a Dorothy Gale any more than she had believed in Oz. She had refused to believe right up until she and Dori found themselves swept up in a tornado and whirled away to the amazing Land of Oz.

Emma believed now. In fact, she was trying to use the snow globe to see what was happening in Oz. Glinda the Good had assured the girls that they could occasionally see their Oz friends in it. Emma didn't know how the magic worked; she just knew that it sometimes did, as long as the girls remembered to say Ozma's name when they looked into the snow globe.

Most of the time it just showed tiny swirls of glinting white flecks around a teeny green model of Princess Ozma's marvelous royal palace in the Emerald City. But sometimes a spark of light glowed deep in the snow globe. When it did, the girls saw it expand until they could see inside the palace—and there would be the Tin Woodman or the Scarecrow or Scraps the Patchwork Girl walking in and out, or playing in the gardens with other famous inhabitants of Oz, or dancing sometimes, with pretty colored lights strung up over the fountains, when Ozma had a party.

Those parties always looked merry, and the sisters

watched them with wistful longing, but there had not been many of them of late.

Em shut out the sound of the wind howling around the corners of their old house and frowned down into the snow globe. "I would like to see what Princess Ozma is doing," she said in a clear voice. "Come on, magic, work today," she added in a whisper.

Was that a spark? No, it was just a reflection of her desk light. No, it wasn't! It *was* a spark! Em watched the pinpoint of light grow into a multicolored glow. She concentrated fiercely on the light in case her wavering attention might somehow douse the magic.

But it brightened steadily until she saw the emerald green lawn behind Ozma's palace, with its splashing fountain. Before it stood an unusual figure made of rosy, polished copper, with a round body and a smaller ball for a head. He was sturdy and motionless as only a mechanical being can be. He gripped a sign in his metal fingers.

Em bent closer, almost touching her nose to the snow globe. She looked at the sign. The letters seemed to dance, then reform into English:

Dori and Em!

"Hey! That's us!" Em looked up in surprise, then turned her gaze back to the sign before her magical view of the Emerald City gardens could vanish.

She bent closer, squinting at the words below her name.

We must consult about Prince Rikiki of the Nome kingdom.

Rik! Em wrinkled her nose. She hadn't really liked that boy. He'd lied far too much, and what's more, he'd obviously enjoyed lying. But Dori had liked him. She said she felt sorry for him, a ragged deposed prince who wanted his kingdom back. She'd also found his lies funny.

Em knuckled her chin with one hand as she peered down into the snow globe. Well, what did the rest of the sign say?

If you wish to come help, tap the snow globe three times.

And it was signed, with a flourish,

Princess Ozma

Ruler of Oz

Go to Oz again? Ozma and Glinda wanted them back? "Hurray!" she breathed.

Even if she had to see Rik, it would be worth it! She set the snow globe on her desk and hurried downstairs to the kitchen, where she smelled the warm, delicious, cinnamony smell of baking oatmeal-and-raisin cookies.

As soon as Dori saw her younger sister race around the corner of the staircase, she knew something was up. Em was ordinarily so practical. Her brown hair was worn short and her serious face and her clothes always chosen for comfort and wear, not for style or beauty. Dori was just the opposite, and before they'd gone to Oz the sisters had not gotten on very well.

Dori prized imagination above just about anything else. She wore her own brown hair long, usually in braids tied with ribbons, or held back with butterfly pins, and she loved pretty clothes. Dori knew she'd be happiest if the fashions of America changed to long, flouncy princess dresses.

Dori paused in the act of spooning cookie batter onto the baking sheet and swiped a wisp of hair off her forehead. Why was Em grinning like that? With Em, it could mean anything from a snow globe vision to a tough math problem solved.

Em glanced around the room to see if they were alone. Mom stood over in the corner by the basement stairs, talking into the phone in a low voice.

"I saw them," Em whispered.

Dori frowned. Her sister's lips were moving, but she had no idea what she was saying.

Em rolled her eyes up toward the ceiling and made sharp motions with her chin.

"Em! Stop making faces at your sister," Mom said as she hung up the phone. "I hope you girls aren't starting that again, not when it's been so nice since summer." Mom looked tired and worried.

"I wasn't making faces," Em began in an injured voice.

"It was just a joke," Dori said quickly. "We weren't teasing or fighting or anything, Mom."

Mom frowned at Em, who was biting her lip. When Mom turned her way, Dori said, "So who was on the phone? I hope this storm hasn't caused anybody problems. It sure sounds nasty outside."

Now Mom's frown changed from irritation to sadness. "There's a problem, but it's not the storm. Though that might make things difficult," she said. Then she sat down at the table, absently pushing aside the cooling cookies Dori had set out. As the sisters watched, Mom put both elbows on the table and rested her forehead in her hands.

They looked at each other. Something was definitely wrong. Mom hated people putting elbows on the table.

"Gran is sick," Mom said. "Aunt Susan just called to say that Gran has checked into the hospital. What she thought was just the flu has turned into pneumonia."

"Oh, poor Gran!" Dori exclaimed.

"I've got to try to reach your father," Mom said, sounding reluctant.

Dad had been living in an apartment ever since the girls' parents separated.

Mom added in a disbelieving tone, "I suppose I'll have to ask him for help."

"Of course Dad will help," Dori said loyally.

Her mom just waved a hand, as though shooing away flies. "This changes all our holiday plans."

Dori exclaimed, "You mean you have to go all the way across the state to Garden City in this weather? And this is our vacation. The first time off since summer! Why can't Aunt Susan go? She doesn't work!"

Em frowned, but didn't say anything.

"I really wanted to spend these two weeks with you girls. . . ." Mom paused and rubbed her eyes. "Aunt Susan is about to fly down to Florida with her entire family. If she has to stay behind, they all do, she says. That's hardly fair when they've paid for their tickets and hotel and everything. And someone has to be there for Gran." She got up and moved back to the phone.

Em motioned toward the oven. "Get those cookies in, Dori, and come upstairs. We have to talk," she added in a meaningful voice.

Dori's fingers shook as she plopped the last of the cookies onto the sheet and then slid it into the hot oven. All her pleasure in baking had vanished. She set the timer and put the bowl and spoon into the sink. Em said impatiently, "I'll wash those. Later. Just come on." The girls left the dishes and ran up the stairs.

Em led the way to her room. As soon as Dori got inside, Em whirled around, shut the door, and stood with her back to it. In a few quick words, she described what she had seen in the snow globe.

Dori's expression changed from surprise to pleasure, then dismay.

Em ended with her own expression of dismay. "Right. But how can we go? Last summer no one noticed we were gone for several days because poor Mom was unconscious in the hospital from that nasty clout on the head."

Both girls remembered the storm that had swept them away to Oz.

"But what are we going to do?" Dori asked. "Princess Ozma needs our help. I don't want to let her down. And I'd love to go back to Oz!"

Em nodded.

"So let's think. I wonder if we could go at night, and come back before morning?" Dori suggested.

Em shook her head. "Mom would notice for sure. You know she checks on us every night."

"I suppose you're right." Dori sighed. "Then what can we—"

A soft knock at the door silenced the girls.

"Come in," Em called.

Mom opened the door and just stood there, leaning against the jamb. Both girls looked at each other. Mother never leaned—she disapproved of leaning. "I'm sorry, girls, I know it won't be any fun spending your vacation in the waiting room of a hospital, but your dad seems to have actually gotten a job interview. Perfect timing."

Dori flushed.

Mom shook her head. "Sorry. I don't mean that. I'm glad he may have a job," she added, sounding not very glad at all. "But he had to go out of town for his interview, and he won't be back until the day after tomorrow. I'll have to take you with me to Garden City."

Em thought quickly. "Why don't we just stay here?" she asked. "We're old enough to take care of ourselves for just a couple of days. Then Dad will be here."

"Oh no. We couldn't do that," Mom said automatically,

but both girls heard the doubt in her voice.

Dori said, "Mom, listen. We can do it. There are neighbors on both sides of us. We have lots and lots of food."

"You could call us every hour or so," Em put in.

"Besides, we're alone every day from when we get home from school until you get home from your work," Dori added. "It's like we've been practicing."

Mom looked from one sister to the other, and the girls could see her wavering.

"We'd be so much happier here," Dori said. "With all our things."

"Much better than sitting around a hospital waiting room all day. You know they won't let us in Gran's room for more than a few minutes," Em said.

"I don't know. . . ."

"Please," both girls said together. Em added, "We promise to be very, *very* responsible."

Mom sighed. "I think—if we set some careful rules—if I call each morning and evening, and if Mrs. Gupta next door agrees to check on you at least once a day, it might be all right. . . ."

Mom went back downstairs, and in a few moments the girls heard her on the phone again.

Dori shut the door, looking excited. "Then we can go!"

Dori had the better imagination of the two, but Em was the more practical.

"No, we can't," she said slowly, hating the words.

Dori's excitement faded.

"What? Why not?"

"With Mom calling all the time, and Mrs. Gupta coming over, and who knows else checking on us? No, I don't see any way for us both to go," Em said, shaking her head. "One of us, maybe."

"One?" Dori said.

"Sure. Here's how I see it. One of us stays to answer the phone and deal with Mrs. Gupta. She can say the other one is upstairs taking a bath, or down in the basement folding laundry, or taking a nap."

Dori groaned. "I don't mind fibbing about that to Mrs. Gupta, but I hate to lie to Mom or Dad."

"So do I," Em said. "But we already have, you know."

Dori flopped down on the bed. "Yes. Well, we didn't actually lie about what happened last summer. We just didn't tell the whole truth."

Em nodded. "We couldn't tell Mom the truth about Oz. She'd never, ever believe us."

Dori rubbed her eyes. She could easily imagine their mother's reaction. Mom liked order and believed only what she could see, touch, taste, and hear. Aunt Susan was even more definite. She called anything that hinted of magic "baby games" and "silly." Mom seemed to become more like Aunt Susan every day. Since Dad had moved out, she almost never smiled or joked anymore, just worked or cleaned. "I want a quiet, orderly life, with a schedule every day and a paycheck each month," she often said.

The girls knew if they claimed they'd been to Oz, Mom

would just hustle them off to a psychiatrist—probably one picked by Aunt Susan—who believed children should be practical, orderly, and useful, to prepare them for a future as practical, orderly, and useful adults.

Em said, "Look, we're not lying to hurt anybody. And Mom worries so much. It's not a bad thing to pretend one of us is here if it keeps Mom from worrying."

"That's true," Dori said slowly. "And we—that is, you or I—will come right back to the house when we find out what Ozma needs our help with."

Em said, "It might be a very short adventure."

"All right," Dori said. "But which of us to go? Should we do rock-paper-scissors? That's only fair."

"It's fair," Em said, nodding. "But we don't need to. I think it ought to be you. I'll stay here, and be the two of us. If Rik is in trouble, you're the one to help him. You're his friend—or the closest thing he has to a friend—and I'm not."

"But you're the practical one," Dori said. "You always think of good ideas."

"So do you," Em said. "Though in a different way. And you know Oz better than I do. You've read all the books several times, and I've only read them once."

So rock-paper-scissors it was, three quick games. Em won the first, Dori the second. On the third Dori shut her eyes, she was so anxious—and didn't see Em change her scissors to a rock, so that Dori's paper would cover it.

"You're it!" Em declared.

Dori didn't answer. She couldn't. She just lunged forward and hugged her sister.

"Go down and get those cookies out before they burn," Em grumped, but the shining look of happiness in her sister's face made her feel she'd done the right thing.

THAT NIGHT Mom was a whirlwind of activity. She flung things into her suitcase, pausing only to either call someone or answer the phone. The next morning, just as the sun came up, a cab arrived right behind the snowplows. Mom gave the girls last-moment hugs and admonitions to mind the rules before the cab took her away to the train station.

Once the girls were alone, they ran back up to Dori's room. As usual, it was adrift in drawings, piles of books, and her porcelain ponies scattered about. Dori tossed her sweater and jeans onto the floor, then rummaged through her messy drawers, pulling out shorts and a summer top.

"What are you doing?" Em asked in blank surprise. "You'll freeze!"

"Not in Oz," Dori said, wrestling into the clothes. "The weather's never nasty there."

Em sighed. "True."

Dori finished dressing and put on her running shoes. "That's that," she said. "I'm ready."

The girls looked at each other. Now that the time had come, they both felt a little reluctant.

Then Em swallowed, squared her shoulders, and held out the snow globe. "It won't get done any faster standing around," she said.

But Dori hesitated, her brown eyes worried. "Are you sure you'll be okay?"

"Of course I will. I have lots of stuff planned!" Em declared, holding out the snow globe for her sister to take.

"What if this goes with me?" Dori asked, cradling the snow globe on her palms. "I want you to be able to watch, if you can."

"Then wish for it to stay here," Em said. "Hurry up!"

Dori held the snow globe on the flat of one palm. She tapped the snow globe three times and wished for it to remain behind with Em.

Sparkling lights glittered all around Dori, whirling faster and faster, and then she disappeared, leaving Em standing alone in the middle of the room.

The snow globe trembled in the air and then fell to the carpet with a thunk.

"It worked!" Em said. Relieved, Em bent and picked up the snow globe and put it in her pocket. Before she left, she gathered an armful of Oz books. The best way to keep her sister company was to read them all again, starting with the very first one.

D ori felt a crazy tingle all over, as if a zillion bees hummed all around her. Just when the hum got so loud she felt she might get stung by them, she blinked and found herself in a garden and the hum was gone. Right before her stood the copper mechanical man.

He closed up his placard and clapped the two ends together, and the whole thing vanished with a blue twinkle. Then he said, "Greet-ings, Prin-cess Oz-ma a-waits."

His voice was flat and mechanical, but somehow friendly. Dori said, "Hi, Tik-Tok. Glad to meet you." She was about to add that it was good to be back, that the garden was beautiful, but she hesitated.

Lovely blossoms of all colors nodded all around, but the light was so strange, not like she remembered at all. Then she looked up and gasped. A thick greenish-gray cloud roiled low overhead. It seemed so low she felt if she reached up, she could touch it.

In the gray and green and brownish vapors, vague, nasty faces seemed to form and then dissolve again. The cloud swirled slowly. The faces came and went, some smirking and all mean, with mouths open, as if yelling awful things.

"Greet-ings, Prin-cess Oz-ma a-waits."

Were there really faces? The vapor misted and billowed, and if she blinked, she saw just thick cloud. But it was the kind of thick, greenish cloud from which lightning might strike. She hunched her shoulders, afraid.

"We will go in-side," Tik-Tok said, marching toward the nearest door leading into the palace. His joints whirred with clockwork precision.

Dori followed his measured footsteps, hurrying away from the troubling cloud.

As soon as they were inside, she breathed a sigh of relief and looked around with great pleasure at the clean, shining marble floors and the sparkling emeralds glittering in graceful carvings over the arched doorways. "Let's find Ozma. I remember those awful clouds from my last visit. Maybe she knows what they are."

"This way," Tik-Tok responded, and led Dori down a hall.

Their steps echoed as they walked. Dori hoped to see familiar Oz people. Where were the Scarecrow, and the Cowardly Lion, and jolly Scraps the Patchwork Girl?

Tik-Tok led Dori not to Ozma's vast throne room as she'd expected, but to a charming parlor that let in the morning sunlight. Dori glanced around at the pretty furnishings, the upholstery and pillows all embroidered in rose and green, and when at last she peeked out the long windows, the sky was blue. The threatening clouds had vanished.

Ozma was sitting in a wing-backed chair, a magic book on her lap. "Hello, Dori," she said.

Dori marveled again at how lovely she was, all dressed

in layers of daintily embroidered rose and gold, her long waving hair held back by a gold coronet. But Dori was most taken with Ozma's face. She was only a teenager, but kindness, wisdom, and a lurking sense of humor showed in the way her eyes crinkled and her cheeks dimpled on either side of her smile. Dori thought her the loveliest person she had ever met.

"I'm so glad to be back," she exclaimed. "But where is everyone?"

Ozma's brows puckered slightly, and her smile turned pensive. "Come, sit down," she replied, "and we can talk."

Dori plopped herself down in the other wing-backed chair, then straightened up. She couldn't slouch in the presence of the ruler of Oz.

Ozma closed her book and laid it aside. "You remember that we thought Princess Dorothy was out traveling, exploring new lands?" she began.

Dori nodded. It had been so strange! Last time she was in Oz, she and Em had met many of Dorothy's friends, and Dori had even borrowed one of Dorothy's beautiful dresses, but they had not once seen Dorothy herself.

Ozma said, "I very much fear that something has happened to her."

"Have you tried to see her in your Magic Picture?" Dori asked. All Ozma had to do was think about a person, wish to see him or her, and there the person would be, pictured in the frame.

"I have." Ozma nodded once. "I saw her sitting very

still, surrounded by . . . gray. Glinda has consulted her *Great Book of Records*, and it only says that 'Dorothy is under a cloud.' "

Dori frowned. Glinda's *Great Book of Records* reported everything happening in Oz, but as is so often the case with magical objects, it did not always work the way you wanted it to. Its wording could be tricky. Some of the entries had been misunderstood in the past.

"Some very powerful magic must be involved, so Glinda is investigating it herself. But she can only investigate the magical side of this mystery," Ozma explained. "Dorothy's friends have all volunteered to make more practical searches. Betsy Bobbin and Trot left together to search all the lands Dorothy often visits, to see if they can pick up clues. The Cowardly Lion is traveling about in the animal kingdoms, to find out if there are clues there. And Scraps set out just yesterday to visit with our friends who were made by magical means, to see if she can discover any news."

Dori said, "Well, I hope they will find Dorothy quickly. Oh! That reminds me. When I got here, one of those terrible clouds was right overhead. Remember, we saw one when I was here last?"

Ozma nodded again, looking concerned. "Those clouds appear here and there, at odd times. Many people have reported seeing them, but they vanish rapidly again, too rapidly to be investigated. Glinda thinks they are just a nuisance."

"I hope they're just a nuisance," Dori said. "Em and I don't like them at all."

"I see that your sister is not here," Ozma observed.

"Yes. Only one of us could come. See, the grown-ups won't believe about Oz back home, so my sister has to stay and pretend both of us are there until I get back. I don't suppose there's some way to fix time so I could get back right after I left?"

"I don't know a way, but that is the sort of magic that Glinda understands best," Ozma said. "Oz is a fairyland, as you know, and so our time marches . . . sideways to yours."

"Sideways." Dori considered that, and nodded. "Yep, even Em would say that makes sense somehow. Well, then I'd better hurry along. It's not fair to keep Em waiting."

Ozma smiled. "You are a good sister."

Dori grinned, flushing. "Em is the good sister. She's the one who stayed at home."

"You are good to come, and she is good to stay," Ozma said diplomatically. "Now, to our problem. You'll remember that Prince Rikiki told us that he wished to reclaim the throne of King Ruggedo, his father. For a long time, it seemed he had forgotten. Glinda checked on him from time to time. After all, Prince Rikiki is a Nome, and they have not always had good intentions toward us. He seemed quite happy exploring some of our more mysterious lands and getting into adventures. But he always worked his way toward the border. And not long ago, he descended to the caverns below the surface, which the Nomes made in order to cross under the Deadly Desert. We believe he is making his way to the Nome kingdom."

Dori said, "He always said he would. Is that a problem?"

"Well, yes and no. I do not interfere with kings and queens outside my borders, and in turn they do not interfere with me. That has worked fine with almost everyone, except the Nomes."

Dori said, remembering what she had read in the Oz books, "Rik's father tried more than once to conquer all of Oz."

"Yes. And both times we were saved when he drank the Waters of Forgetfulness." Ozma pointed out the window toward the deceptively pretty fountain whose magical waters erased all memory. King Roquat had gathered a lot of nasty allies and dug a way under the Deadly Desert in order to come conquering. But his tunnel had come out by that very fountain. The king and his chieftains had paused for a drink before embarking on their terrible plans—and had promptly forgotten not only those plans, but who they were. He'd changed his name to Ruggedo and gone back to his caves. But later he made another try at invading Oz, and drank from the Forbidden Fountain again—this time disappearing to a quiet life. No one knew where.

Kaliko, Roquat's chief steward, had taken over the Nome throne. He was not exactly a model of goodness, but at least he had shown no signs of wanting to venture outside his borders—yet. You could never tell with Nomes.

"Would it be so bad if Rik reclaims his throne?" Dori asked.

"Who sits on the throne of the Nomes is their business. What I am afraid of is that Prince Rikiki's reappearance in the Nome kingdom might cause war with their neighbors," Ozma responded.

"You think Rik might cause a war?" Dori asked.

"No," Ozma said. "But some of the Nomes' neighbors are very wicked, and war is never a good thing for anyone. Yet I dare not interfere in Nome affairs, for Kaliko might take that as a sign that he can come here and interfere in Oz."

"Yuk," Dori exclaimed. "I hadn't thought of that."

"This dilemma has caused me to ponder deeply. Here is what I think is the best plan. From what Glinda has told me, Prince Rikiki seems to put little trust in adults. Prince Inga of Pingaree is more or less his age and has had experience with the Nomes. He's already skilled at diplomacy. I could send him to Prince Rikiki to find out what his intentions are. But Rikiki might not welcome Prince Inga if he were just to appear alone."

Dori, picturing the wary, distrustful Rik, nodded firmly. "Oh, I think you're right."

"But you managed to make friends with him. You also offered to help him, and he did not reject your promise, either, if I remember rightly?"

"No, he didn't," Dori said.

"So if you accompany Prince Inga, it might make the mission more acceptable to Prince Rikiki. The two of you can use your wits and strengths to circumvent war, whichever person claims the throne of the Nome kingdom."

"I'll do it," Dori exclaimed.

Ozma smiled her lovely smile and reached forward to hug Dori. "Oh, thank you. I felt sure that you would help. Well, then, as your sister *is* waiting back in Kansas for your return, perhaps I ought to summon the flying carpet at once to get you safely over the Deadly Desert."

"I'm ready to go," Dori said stoutly, though secretly wishing she could spend just a little more time in the Emerald City.

Within a few minutes, Ozma had made the arrangements. Then the two girls walked out into a garden with lilies growing in all shades of the rainbow. When Ozma and Dori looked up, there was no sign of that terrible cloud. The sky was the pretty robin's egg blue that you expected to see in Oz.

The magic carpet arrived, and behind it came Jellia Jamb, Ozma's steward. "I thought you might enjoy this," said Jellia, smiling at Dori as she hoisted a picnic basket onto the carpet.

"Oh, thank you," Dori said, realizing that she'd forgotten to eat before she'd left Kansas. She stared hungrily at the basket.

"Skipped your breakfast?" Jellia Jamb chuckled. "I'm used to the ways of adventurers."

Dori sat down in the center of the red carpet. She was well acquainted with it from her previous adventure. "To the royal castle of Pingaree!" she said.

The carpet swooped up into the air, leaving Princess Ozma and Jellia Jamb far below, waving and smiling.

DORI HAD CROSSED OZ twice before from the air, once on this same carpet and another time carried by the Winged Monkeys. She looked down eagerly, hoping to spot valleys and mountains both familiar and strange.

So many mysterious places made up the four countries of Oz. How she'd love to explore them all! But as she gazed down, the whole land below suddenly fell under a deep shadow.

Dori turned around and saw a big gray cloud filling the sky. As she watched, it seemed to grow, until she could see faint greenish edgings of distorted faces. Then she realized it was not growing—it was coming closer.

She flung herself flat on the carpet and gasped out, "Faster, carpet. As fast as you can." She curled her arms around the picnic basket as the carpet vibrated beneath her and began to pick up speed.

Wind whistled overhead and all around the edges of the carpet. She dug her face into its pile, which smelled pleasantly like her sun-dried woolen bedspread back home. It gave her a comforting sense of safety. Was that feeling of safety real? She lifted her lead and peered over her shoulder. The ominous cloud was now dwindling rapidly in the distance, leaving Oz under sunshine and blue skies.

"Phew!" Dori said. She sat up shakily and looked down once more. She was flying over the terrible sands of the Deadly Desert, upon which no living being could set foot. There was not much to see except miles and miles of sand, so instead she turned her attention to the basket of fresh fruit and tasty little sandwiches that Jellia Jamb had packed.

By the time she finished her meal, Dori saw a line of green in the east. Yes! There straight ahead were the mighty mountains under which the Nome kingdom lay. She shifted around on the carpet and shaded her eyes, trying to remember what she had read about the country below. There in the north lay the Kingdom of Ev. The main entrance to the Nome kingdom was on the border of Ev.

Dori looked to the south. Off in the distance were two really creepy kingdoms. The Phanfasms lived on the southern border of the Nome kingdom. Those Phanfasms had once allied with the Nomes against Ozma. Beyond them was the strange and mysterious Kingdom of Dreams. She thought she saw a low mist covering that land.

Before too long the imposing mountains gradually eased into green, rolling hills, on which could be seen villages, a patchwork of farms, and here and there a turreted and towered castle. Now she must be flying over the land of jolly King Rinkitink, who had gone with Prince Inga on his adventure into the land of the Nomes. Beyond his kingdom was a stretch of bright blue that swiftly resolved into the Nonestic Ocean. The water was so bright and so deep it looked purple when she flew right over it. And soon she saw a bump on the horizon that, as she approached, revealed itself to be the Island of Pingaree.

The carpet banked gently and started its descent. It was late afternoon now, and the slanting sunlight glinted in the emerald leaves of the trees that grew all across the island. From above, Pingaree looked almost uninhabited, but Dori knew that those big, spreading trees hid the houses.

There was no city on this little island. The only visible dwelling was at the north end, toward which the carpet now flew. The palace of King Kitticut and Queen Garee, Prince Inga's parents, was built of white marble, with glowing domes of burnished gold. It truly looked like a royal palace.

The carpet settled directly onto a broad terrace of polished marble tiles. Dori had just enough time to hop off, clutching her empty picnic basket, and look around in wonder at the fluted columns and high archways, before a pair of stately stewards appeared.

Despite the fact that she had been sent by Princess Ozma on an important errand, Dori felt intimidated by these tall, stern-faced fellows in their impressive uniforms. But then a shorter figure came running between them and stopped, smiling in welcome.

It was a boy, dressed like a prince ought to be dressed— in a fine velvet tunic with a golden coat of arms stitched across the chest, pantaloons, and shiny boots with tassels at the high tops. His light-colored hair was longish and curled around his handsome face under a velvet cap with a long feather clasped on by a golden circlet set with a pearl.

"Hullo," he said. "I saw your carpet from my tower."

"Are you Prince Inga?" Dori asked.

In answer, he swept off his cap and bowed, an elegant bow performed with a princely air. Dori was totally unused to boys bowing, much less wearing feathered velvet caps, and she repressed the urge to giggle. Inga looked friendly, but would a prince like being laughed at? She rather suspected not.

"I'm Dori," she managed, with no more than a single tremor in her voice, and if Inga thought it was timidity, he was welcome to that thought. "Ozma sent me."

Inga's brows rose. "Ah. State business, then. Please, come this way. My royal parents will wish to hear what you have to say."

"All right," Dori agreed, but before she could move, one of the tall attendants cleared his throat.

Dori looked up.

"Shall I take the basket, miss?" he asked, and held out his hand.

Dori handed it over. "Very well, but mind, when I return to Princess Ozma it has to go with me, because it rightly belongs to Jellia Jamb."

The man bowed; the two stewards turned about and moved away noiselessly. Dori skipped to catch up to Prince Inga. He marched with long, boyish strides down a high-ceilinged hall lined with huge tapestries, and into a fabulous throne room. Dori admired the golden chandeliers, the giant portraits of former kings and queens, and the twin canopied—but empty—thrones. "Nobody there," Inga said. "Of course! The farewell luncheon must just be ending."

"Farewell luncheon?" Dori asked, glancing out the window at the setting sun.

"Yes, but it does run a bit long. There's always some entertainment, and then a lot of gift giving and rewards, and by the time the things are handed round, and everyone makes speeches, the day almost disappears before the guests do."

"Who are they saying farewell to?" Dori asked.

"Oh, courtiers," Inga said, as he cocked his head. "Yes, I hear them out by the stable, saying good-bye. You see, because we are an island, we are too small to have an entire class of nobility in the way other, bigger kingdoms do, so the people of Pingaree take turns being courtiers. That way

it never gets too boring, having to wear your best clothes
and use your best manners all the time. People stay until
they have seen all the current plays at least twice, and until
the balls and parties make their feet hurt, and then they go
back to their oyster farming, and next day a fresh crop of
volunteers shows up for their turn."

"Now that sounds like a fine idea," Dori said.
"Everybody gets to be a duke or duchess for as long as they
like?"

"Yes, that's the idea," Inga agreed. "My mother's third
sister, my favorite aunt, says that her stomach can only
stand duchess food a couple of months of the year."

Just then two uniformed attendants threw back a pair
of great carved doors to admit two tall figures. Entering
first was a man in gold-edged robes, followed by a woman
in a long, sweeping dress of brocaded silk. Dori didn't need
to see the golden crowns on their heads to guess that she
was meeting King Kitticut and Queen Garee.

"Inga, dear," the queen said, smiling at Dori. "Have we
a visitor?"

"Yes, Mother. Sent by Princess Ozma of Oz," Inga
replied.

The king and queen looked serious at once.

"Well then, young lady," King Kitticut said to Dori.
"You have arrived betimes. We have just sent off our
departing courtiers, and the new ones do not arrive until
morning. We have the evening in which to discuss state
affairs."

State affairs. Dori loved the sound of that. Only in Oz and its neighbors, she reflected, could a kid be included in a discussion of state affairs.

The king led the way to an airy chamber with a big map of the Island of Pingaree on one wall.

They all sat in high-backed carved chairs, the cushions' deep red velvet all embroidered with lilies. At the center of each was a tiny pearl, set in a pucker so that sitting wasn't uncomfortable. Each chair had a crown carved on its high back.

"Now, my dear," the queen said in a kindly voice. "Would you like to tell us who you are, and why our good friend Ozma, Princess of Oz, has sent you to us?"

Dori introduced herself, and then in a few quick words (she'd already thought it all out during the ride on the flying carpet) she described Rik's quest and Ozma's reasons for wishing to send Dori along to help.

At the end, both royal parents nodded. The king said, "I can certainly understand her concerns. A civil war among the Nomes would be a terrible thing—not just for them, but also for everyone around their border. They have some . . . restless, shall we say?—yes, *restless* neighbors who would love a chance to get in a spot of warfare, especially on someone else's territory."

"Yet I worry about sending two young people," the queen said to her husband. "You remember our own terrible experiences there. I still have nightmares about it."

"Very true, my dear. Still, it was a young person,

Princess Dorothy, who came to our rescue."

"But if what Miss Dori says is true, Princess Dorothy may be in danger herself nowadays. This bodes ill, I fear," the queen said, her fingers fiddling with the long rope of diamonds and emeralds hanging around her neck.

"Yes, but it is the duty of a ruler to take risks," the king pointed out.

"Risks for his own people, I agree," the queen replied, "but for the Nomes?" She turned to Inga and Dori. "Perhaps, my son, you might take our visitor on a tour of the palace while your father and I discuss what must be done?"

Prince Inga rose and bowed to his royal parents. Dori rose too, wondered if she ought to curtsey, and then remembered that she was an American and Americans don't bow. So she nodded politely and followed Inga from the room. Before the doors shut behind them, the low-voiced murmurs of the royal parents started up again.

"Oh, I hope you can go with me," Dori exclaimed. "I'll go alone if I have to, but I'd so much rather have company."

Inga smiled. "If Princess Ozma wishes me to accompany you, then it will be so. It will just take my mother some time to talk herself around to it," he explained. "Sudden changes worry her. But look. It is sunset. Let me show you something I believe you will like."

They ran up the winding staircase that led to the top of one of the towers. As she followed behind the athletic prince, Dori reflected that even living in a castle one couldn't get out of shape, not with all these stairs to climb and those long halls.

They emerged in one of the golden domes. There were windows all around, affording a splendid view of the island and the sparkling sea. Inga stepped back, looking at Dori expectantly. She gazed out at the deep blue of the ocean and sucked in a slow breath of delight. After a long moment, she began to turn away.

"Oh, but wait," Inga said. "Keep watching."

Dori turned back. "For wh—" she began, then stopped.

Out just beyond the waves, water splashed up into a rainbow-hued spray as it caught the slanting rays of the setting sun. Through the splash shot the figure of a girl, or half of a girl.

A mermaid!

She leaped up into the air, fishtail quivering, her arms outspread, her long, waving hair flowing out. Dori could see the golden light of sunset on her laughing face.

"That's the daughter of the queen of mermaids," said Inga.

The mermaid princess dove back into the sea, then leaped up again. Suddenly there were splashes all around her. Young merfolk shot high into the air and then dove down again. Graceful silver dolphins circled the merfolks, flying up, arcing through the air, and splashing down in perfect formation.

Two, three more times they performed their aerial

dance, and then the merpeople disappeared back in their watery realm.

"Sometimes I take my sailboat out onto the water, and they dance all around me," Inga said. "They do it at dawn and sunset. Isn't it grand?"

Dori clasped her hands. "It's the loveliest thing I ever saw in my life!"

"We have a special sort of alliance with the queen of the mermaids," Inga said as they started back down the long spiral staircase. "Our main export is pearls, which are the finest within many kingdoms. But we are careful to only take the ones our oyster beds offer, and no more. That keeps peace with our friends in the deeps. We are also on the watch for less trustworthy neighbors on other islands. In turn, the mermaid queen once gave us something we value more than gold or palaces, something we keep very secret. But I think my mother is going to insist we use them, so I had better tell you about our three magic pearls."

Dori nodded. She had read all about the pearls in the Oz books, of course, but she figured it was only polite to let Inga tell her in his own way.

"Each pearl has a different magical power," said Inga. "They were a big help to Princess Dorothy and me on our last adventure with the Nomes, in fact."

They reached the throne room, where the king and queen were waiting.

King Kitticut said, "We have talked it over, my son. Miss Dori."

Queen Garee, a motherly-looking woman despite all her silks and jewels, said, "In truth, we would not permit anyone to go anywhere near those terrible Nomes by choice. But if Princess Ozma thinks it right, we must agree."

"We know that any friend of Princess Ozma will come equipped with the same valor and wit that Princess Dorothy exhibited when she came to our aid," the king said.

Inga gave Dori a quick grin.

"My husband is right," Queen Garee said earnestly. "And yet, we would feel better if you would also take along the three magic pearls for protection, as Princess Dorothy once did."

"Princess Dorothy was willing to use them," the king said, also looking very earnest, "so there can be no imputation of lack of courage or honor."

Dori felt a sigh starting somewhere down inside her toes. Kings and queens could talk all they wanted about valor and suchlike, but as far as she was concerned, it was always better to go into danger with as much help as you could get.

The king brought out a little bag, which he opened in a solemn manner. He shook out three shiny pearls, one white, one pink, and one blue.

"These are our mightiest protection," he said to Dori. "The white pearl will give good advice. The pink pearl will keep you from harm. The blue pearl will give you great strength. We send these with you."

"Thank you," Dori and Inga said together as the king put the pearls back into the bag, then handed it to his son.

The four of them presently had a splendid supper served out on one of the terraces. Twelve courses were borne in and out on golden platters as the king and queen alternated between offering Inga and Dori good advice and relating stories about the Nomes.

Afterward Dori was offered a royal-sized bed in which a family of six could easily have slept. She resisted the impulse to bounce on the bed like a trampoline, figuring that this sort of behavior would not be welcome at a royal palace, and snuggled down between silken sheets to sleep.

The next morning Dori and Inga joined the king and queen for a fabulous breakfast. Dori had never seen so many kinds of fruits, pies and tarts, and fancy breads, all offered on golden plates.

When Dori was stuffed, the king said, "The day is well advanced and it is time for you to depart."

"We arranged for a picnic," the queen said, her voice trembling. "Oh dear! You will be careful, won't you?"

"We promise, Mother dear," Inga said, kissing her cheek.

His father clapped him on the back and Inga turned to Dori, surreptitiously glancing at the door, as if to say *Let's get moving.* The queen fumbled for a lace-edged handkerchief embroidered with golden crowns and began to dab at her eyes.

The king and queen walked them to the magic carpet, which lay waiting for them on the grand terrace. As Inga and Dori climbed on, one of the tall stewards appeared and handed them Jellia Jamb's basket, crammed with goodies.

Inga, seeing his mother start to sniffle, said grandly, and a little hastily, "Rise, carpet, and away for the Kingdom of Ev!"

BACK IN KANSAS, Em woke in a quiet house. Outside her window the snowstorm was still a curtain of white hiding the houses across the street.

She got up and made breakfast, taking a book with her to keep her company. She had finished *The Wonderful Wizard of Oz* and was starting on *The Marvelous Land of Oz*.

No sooner had she taken a bite of her toast than the phone rang. Her heart started pounding as she picked up the receiver. "Hello?"

"Em? Is that you?" Mom said.

"Sure is. I'm down here having breakfast. Dori's, um, up in Oz." Em had thought her words clever, right until she said them. Then she winced.

"Oh dear," Mom said. "Are you girls quarreling again?"

"No, Mom," Em said hastily. "Everything is as quiet and peaceful as if you were here. No problems at all! How is Gran?"

"She's still very ill," Mom said, sounding tired and worried. "But the medicine ought to begin working today, the doctor said."

"Give her our hugs and kisses," Em replied.

"I will. Bye, dear, and remember, call me if you have the slightest worries or problems," Mom said. She made a kissing noise and hung up.

Phew! That went okay, Em thought—but then the phone rang again. She stood there staring at it as if it had turned into an octopus.

It rang again, and she made herself pick it up. "Hello?"

"Emma! How's my girl?"

"Hi, Dad!"

"Are you girls all right? Where's your sister?"

Gulp. "Well, Dori is kinda busy right now. . . ."

"Doing another of her elaborate drawings, eh? Good, good. Listen, I ought to be there tomorrow, but I'm a little worried about this storm forecast. It looks like a real bad one is coming in. Would you tell your mom, in case something happens and I get stuck here in Nebraska?"

"Sure," Em said, thinking: I just won't say *when* I'll tell her. "Take care, Dad."

He hung up.

Em was just finishing the dishes when the phone rang for the third time. Em groaned and almost didn't pick it up, but she knew how worried her parents would be if it was either of them.

This time it was Mrs. Gupta from next door, and Em assured her that both she and Dori were busy and happy, and that there weren't any problems. She hated lying to her parents, but she didn't mind saying "we" to Mrs. Gupta.

After that Em flopped into a chair. She looked around the quiet kitchen. Weak winter light glowed blue-gray in the window, and the wind howled around the eaves. Inside, everything was just as quiet as she'd told her mother it was.

Too quiet.

No, don't think like that. Keep busy! Then time will pass faster. So what to do first?

She decided to vacuum the living room, then wash the floors, so when Mom returned everything would be in perfect order, to make up for the fibbing.

But before that she'd just take a look in the snow globe.

She ran upstairs and plopped down onto her bed, the snow globe in her hands. Dori always liked to shake it up first, as if the little bits inside actually helped the magic, but Em liked to keep it clear.

"Princess Ozma, please show me Oz," Em stated.

The spark!

Glittering bits of light fluttered inside the glass, resolving into the Emerald City. There were the gardens, and the big, beautiful throne room. Em saw Princess Ozma sitting on her throne, but she was alone.

Em pressed her nose against the cool glass, searching the corners of the throne room, which grew more shadowy. No sign of Dori. Em lowered the snow globe, disappointed. She realized she didn't really want to see Ozma unless Dori was with her.

Where was Dori?

Em had been about to put the snow globe on a shelf, but she stopped and frowned. The girls had never tried to see anything but the Emerald City before. She didn't know if the snow globe's wayward magic would work or not, but she decided to try.

So once again she took the snow globe in both hands, and this time she said, "Princess Ozma, I don't want to see the Emerald City now. What I really, really wish is to see Dori."

And—was that the spark again?

The light inside the glass expanded steadily. Em watched, scarcely daring to breathe. Instead of the beautiful emerald palace, Em stared in delight at two figures on a little square of red, flying high above a bright blue ocean.

There was Dori! Who was that with her? A boy in fancy clothes. She wondered if he was someone from the Oz books.

Em watched the carpet floating gently toward some mountains. Then the light gradually faded and went dark, leaving her staring down at the usual little model of the Emerald City.

Now that she had seen Dori was okay, Em realized she felt a whole lot better about being alone.

She smiled as she got out the vacuum.

5

DORI AND PRINCE INGA
sailed high over the violet-blue waters of the Nonestic
Ocean. It was quite a pleasant journey. The morning sun
was behind them, lighting up the spectacular mountain
range before them.

They had no idea, of course, that Em was watching
them—just as Em did not know that there were other eyes
also observing that scarlet carpet crossing the sky. Those
eyes were both alert and malicious.

Inga and Dori felt quite safe, so high in the sky. The
royal cook of Pingaree had stuffed Jellia Jamb's basket with
more of those fancy breads and tarts from breakfast, plus
an amazing variety of fruits, some of which Dori had never
seen. She wanted to try them all.

Dori and Prince Inga sailed high over the
violet-blue waters of the Nonestic Ocean.

Inga saw her looking at the basket and grinned. "Shall we?"

"Okay," Dori said, and they had a splendid picnic as they sailed over the ocean.

Dori finished last with a fruit Inga told her had been imported from the Gillikin land. It was purple, crunchy, and sweet. After swallowing a juicy bite, she said, "We sure don't have these in Kansas."

"Where is Kansas?" Inga asked.

Dori shrugged. "I can find it on the map at home, but from here, who knows? I always come by magic. Not that we have any at home," she added hastily. "Magic, that is. Glinda the Good arranges it."

"No magic! Then how do you live?"

Dori whiled away some time describing her life in Kansas. She talked about school, and newspapers, and computers, and freeways—until she noticed that Inga's expression never changed. He listened with great politeness, and she thought, *Either it sounds boring, or he can't even imagine these things—they don't sound real to him.*

She hoped it was the latter. Perhaps she'd always thought of home as boring too, but somehow it's different when someone else does.

She stopped talking, discovered she still had an appetite, and busied herself with a honey-custard pastry.

"Ah, there is the coast," Inga said presently. "That is the Land of Ev. It is a most pleasant place."

"You've visited there?"

"Oh yes. My father sent me on a tour. Prince Evardo of Ev was an excellent host. I do not believe we were indoors once but to eat our meals," Inga added with a grin.

Dori liked that grin. It made Inga look a little less imposing and princely and more like a normal person.

But then his smile faded, and he looked stern and princely again. "There, to the south, is Mount Phantastico. Do you see it, sticking up on the horizon?"

Dori grimaced. "Yes. It looks just as awful as it looked when I spotted it yesterday. I was glad the carpet didn't go anywhere near."

"You know about the Phanfasms, then?"

"I do indeed. I know they are much more dangerous than the Nomes. They can change shape. They prefer big scary bodies with animal heads."

"Their greatest delight is bringing sorrow and dismay to others," Inga said.

"Maybe you can tell me something that I don't know," said Dori. "Who lives in the Land of Dreams?"

Inga frowned. "That is a mystery, but I can tell you this: even the Phanfasms are very careful not to cross the border into that land. For whoever goes in never comes out again."

"That sounds really creepy!" Dori said.

"If you please," Prince Inga asked politely. "Would you tell me a little about this Prince Rikiki?"

"You didn't meet him when you were underground in the Nome caves, trying to rescue your parents?"

"The Nomes hide their children," Inga said. "I never

met him, or anyone younger than adult age."

Dori nodded, reflecting that at least Rik had told her the truth about that.

"Well, Rik is a Nome, and that means he doesn't really trust anyone. He tells lies sometimes, but I know that's the way he was raised," Dori added. "I thought he was fun. I kind of liked him."

"But he might not completely welcome our diplomatic mission. Do you agree?"

"Oh, yes," Dori said.

Inga pulled the silk bag from a pocket of his grand tunic and reached into it. His head cocked a little, as if he were listening, and then he gave a short nod. "The white pearl has made a suggestion. Permit me, of your courtesy, to request you to carry this blue pearl. You might, if you agree, conceal it somewhere about in your . . ." Inga looked at Dori's clothes, and finished with a shade of doubt, "garments."

Dori took the pearl, repressing the urge to laugh. Of course, Inga was used to fancy clothes— velvets and sweeping trains and the like. But Dori wasn't a princess, and though she wished she could dress like one sometimes, she wouldn't want to go dragging about in one of those big skirts on an adventure.

She was still smiling at the thought of American summer clothes looking weird to a prince as she slid the blue pearl into her shoe.

Then she heard a rhythmic *Thud! Thump! Thud*!

Inga gasped. "The Iron Giant!"

The Iron Giant was a huge robot, made of plates of iron, standing two hundred feet tall.

They both stared down in considerable dismay. The Iron Giant was a huge robot, made of plates of iron, standing two hundred feet tall. Its tremendous iron feet were planted on either side of a narrow pathway into the mountain, and every couple of seconds it smashed a great iron mallet onto the ground—closing the path between the two cliffs. The mallet came down with terrifying speed, preventing anything from getting through those huge legs and into the caves.

Thump! Boom! Thud!

Dori spotted a familiar thin, tattered figure standing in the middle of the pathway, hands on his hips.

"Rik," Dori called in greeting.

The carpet settled just behind Rik. His slanty brows slanted up even farther when he turned his head and saw Dori.

"I promised to help you get your kingdom back," Dori said, and waved at Inga. "And I brought along a helper. My sister couldn't come."

"Helper?" Rik repeated, looking askance at Inga.

The Prince of Pingaree swept off his hat (this one very sensibly did not have a feather in it, but it was still velvet) and made his fine bow. "Inga of Pingaree," he said. "Pleased to meet you."

"Hah," Rik replied, arms now crossed.

Dori couldn't help comparing them. They were about the same size, more or less, though Inga's shape made it clear he'd one day be brawny, and Rik would always have spindly arms and legs. Inga's clothes and hair were shining and neat, his features princely. Rik, gray skinned as a stone, looked more ragged than ever. His wispy hair stuck out over his ears.

Dori realized she'd missed that challenging grin of his. She said, "So have you been having fun, traveling about?"

Rik laughed. "Hoo! Haven't I just!"

"Do you still have those purple slippers that make the wearer invisible?"

Rik's grin turned into a scowl. "No. Worse luck. I lost 'em during a tangle with—on an adventure." He paused, with a look at Inga. "There'll be time enough to gabble about that." He cupped his hands around his mouth. "Klik! I know you're in there! Let me by!"

Dori frowned, trying to remember which story he was in. "Who's Klik again?"

"The grand chamberlain," Inga and Rik said together. They glanced at each other, Inga apologetic and Rik glowering.

"Oh, yes!" Dori snapped her fingers. "Wears a golden chain. So there's a way in around this awful Iron Giant?" The mallet came down again with a *BOOM*.

"Of course. For Nomes," Rik said. "But the old villain seems to be asleep. He isn't releasing the spell."

"Well, then," Dori said, remembering her pearl. "I did say I was here to help. Allow me."

She marched right up to the giant. Her heart started going bumpety-bump twice as fast as the mallet, but she hid her reaction and put out her hands just as the mallet came down with a smack!

It wasn't a loud smack, just like clapping hands. Dori felt the magic flash all the way through her, and there she stood, holding that mallet as the Iron Giant strained to smash it all the way down.

"Go on," she said, gesturing to the others with her chin.

Rik stared at her in amazement, then gave a long, low whistle. "Why didn't you do something like that when the Witch had us prisoner?"

Dori just shrugged.

Inga and Rik scrambled beneath the huge mallet, Inga giving Dori a smile and Rik glowering in distrust at the mallet as they passed.

Dori turned her head the other way and said past her shoulder, "Carpet, if you work underground, please come."

The carpet vibrated, then resettled.

Dori sighed. "I thought so. Well, then, please stay until we call you, and thanks." She did not know if the carpet had personality with its magic, or just the magic, but it didn't hurt to be nice.

She eased under the mallet herself, then let it go. It smashed down, *THUD*, behind her.

So why hadn't Klik the chamberlain heard Rik?

Because at that moment he was slipping and sliding down the passageway to the great caverns that comprised

King Kaliko's underground palace, with his two best spies tumbling after him.

All three burst into Kaliko's throne room, surprising the king so much he bobbled the hot coal he'd just pulled from his pocket.

"Eh? What's this?"

"Sorry, O Majesty," Klik said, hastily bowing.

Kaliko bent and retrieved the hot coal, put it to his long pipe, and puffed it alight. Then he stuck the coal back into his pocket and eyed the three before him from under his wispy, curling eyebrows. "Well?"

"Rikiki is back," Klik said, nearly out of breath.

"Oh, I always thought he'd return," Kaliko said cheerfully.

"But—"

"I knew he'd soon be sick of that disgusting sunshine, and that nasty air all smelly with things like those irritating and useless flowers."

"But—"

Now he will be more than ready to take up his proper place with the boys down in the mines, learning how to carve gems," Kaliko said with a pleasant chuckle.

"But—well, no," Klik said, looking unhappy.

Kaliko frowned. "No?"

His smile faded as three heads slowly shook back and forth.

"No," said Klik.

"No," said the Long-Eared Hearer, who could hear a fly a mile away.

. . . he . . . eyed the three before him . . .

"No," said the Lookout, who could see that same fly *two* miles away.

"Well, then," Kaliko said, flinging his pipe into a corner. "What's the boy back for?"

"To regain his throne," Klik said.

"What? He never had it in the first place!"

"He has two helpers with him. One of whom, a little girl, is stronger than the Iron Giant."

"A little girl!"

"Yes."

"Stronger than the Giant?"

"Stopped the mallet with just her hands. Didn't even break a sweat," the Lookout said.

"It isn't . . . Dorothy, is it?" Kaliko whispered, looking around fearfully as if he expected monsters to pop out of the rock walls—or even worse than monsters, one little girl with a bright, happy face, dainty clothes, and a big, friendly smile.

"No." All three shook their heads vigorously.

"Phew." Kaliko slumped back on his throne. "Let me think."

"They're on their way up the trail right now," Klik added.

"Well then, let me think fast," Kaliko said. "Huh!" He grinned. "And I was complaining about boredom. Well, well. Thinking fast reminds me of the bad old days, when I was constantly dodging gemstones, rocks, coals, and the royal crown. Old Ruggedo did have a good arm. And here's his son, wanting that same crown. Hmm . . . hmm. . . ."

The three waited a time, then the Long-Eared Hearer tipped one of his long, pointy ears, and said, "They're just outside the entrance cave."

The Lookout squinted upward, each of his bright, cold eyes looking in different directions, and said, "Yes, I see them."

"Ah!" Kaliko said, raising a finger. "Listen. I have a plan."

While Kaliko was describing his plan, Rik was pushing his way through a narrow crack. "This way," he said to the others.

Dori followed easily, and Inga with a bit more difficulty, for he was the largest. But he squeezed through, then brushed off his fine velvet clothes with a faint air of regret.

Rik snorted. "When you're quite happy about your appearance," he said, "we'll move along."

"Your pardon," Inga replied, bowing.

"Huh." Rik shouldered past, then pointed at a dark hole. "In there."

"It's dark," Dori said.

"So it is," Rik said, frowning. "Usually we have magical lights. But then no one comes up much this way. Nomes hate light and wind. Maybe the spell wore out. But it's just a tunnel slide. We don't need to see."

"All right," Inga said. "Why don't you lead the way?"

For answer Rik sauntered to the hole, looked back with

a derisive grin, and dove through with a whoop.

"I guess I'll go next," said Dori.

She eased into the hole, felt smoothed rock, tipped herself over the lip, and began sliding down, down, down.

She heard Inga right behind her.

Whoosh! Cool air ruffled her face and clothes. She zipped around a curve, skimmed around another curve, and then dropped so fast she felt her stomach scrunching.

They popped out, one, two, three. Rik landed on his feet with ease, bending a little and putting his long hands on his skinny knees.

Dori and Inga staggered forward a few steps, arms flailing, until they stopped.

Then both gazed around in complete surprise. They had stopped on a little natural balcony, with a narrow, rocky trail leading directly down to a city made all of glass. Way up above, six colored gemstones glowed like underground suns, giving off a pearly sort of light.

"This isn't the Nome kingdom," Inga breathed.

"No, it isn't," Rik snarled. "Kaliko tricked us!"

I tricked them," Kaliko said, chuckling as he settled back on his throne.

"You didn't turn them into tree stumps?" Klik asked, looking aghast.

"You didn't throw them into the deepest dungeon?" the Long-Eared Hearer asked, flapping his hears in disgust.

"You just . . . sent them away?" the Lookout asked, hopping from one foot to the other in his disappointment.

Kaliko glowered at them all. They promptly stumbled back three or four steps. Then he said, "This is why I am king and not you." He counted on his fingers. "You can't kill anyone in Oz, so I can't get rid of Rik and his companions the easy way. Tree stumps have a way of changing back into whatever they were meant to be when you are least expecting it. And we don't *have* any deepest dungeons. Why would we have deepest dungeons? Deepest dungeons mean someone has to slog all the way down there with food and water every day. Unless you are volunteering for the duty?" He glared at his minions.

"Not me!"

"Not me!"

"Not me!"

"I thought so. And finally, yes, I sent them a long, long way away, to a cavern inhabited by the most annoying people I could think of. It'll take a lot of luck and more hard work to toil all the way back here, and when did Rik ever keep a single idea in mind longer than a day or two? He's gone, and we can relax." Kaliko sat back, chuckling. "All that magic made me hungry. Where is my royal dinner?"

6

THE GLASS CITY was amazing, all tall spires and domed buildings. The smooth glass threw back the light of the six "suns" so that the entire city shimmered with light that changed gently: now rose, now green, now violet, now gold.

But—

"I know this place," Dori said, looking around slowly. "And if I'm right, it's not good."

Inga opened his hands. "I do not know where we are."

Rik made a sour face. He looked especially sour since the light at that moment changed to a deep green. "Nor do I."

Dori looked at him in surprise. "You don't know all the neighboring underground kingdoms?"

"Of course not," Rik said, hands on hips. "Too many of 'em. I only know the ones whose main sport is attacking Nomes." He grinned briefly. "Never heard of this place. What is it, anyway?"

Dori said, "I think we're in the Land of the Mangaboos. Let's get out of here. Walk fast. We won't be able to run."

Both boys gave her puzzled glances. Rather than explain, Dori demonstrated. She began to lope, but as soon as her feet left the ground, she floated into the air. It took her several long moments to come down.

"Hoo," said Rik.

"That is a problem," Inga stated. "If we need to move swiftly."

"Watch this," Dori said with a grin. She lifted her leg as if she were about to climb up stairs. As she stepped, her foot sank down very slowly through the air. She lifted the other foot and stepped higher. She climbed faster than she sank, and when she stopped, she was well above the boys' heads. "We could go all the way there, if we wanted." She pointed to the glass towers above, glowing with softly changing color.

"But no running," Rik muttered. "I can see why the older Nomes—and our warlike neighbors—have never mentioned this place. You couldn't very well conquer it, having to stroll slower than a very lazy snail."

"I think the magic is to protect their glass," Dori said. "They don't like their glass broken, because it grows back slowly. They got mad at Dorothy Gale and the Wizard when they fell down on it." She pointed up at what would have been the sky. The ceiling of the mighty cavern was so high above them they couldn't really see it, only those six colored lights. "Their magic doesn't seem to prevent anything from dropping down from the surface. Even coming down slowly, rocks and big heavy things break their glass. They must hate anything coming from above."

Rik couldn't resist trying to dash straight up, his arms windmilling, in order to perform slow flips and handsprings in the air. Dori watched, laughing, as the slowly changing light painted his ragged clothing with yellow, then deep purple, then orange.

Inga watched for a moment, but he was distracted by a distorted flicker in a glass wall nearby.

He stepped carefully around the wall and gazed down a pathway between the glass buildings.

At a sedate pace, a group of Mangaboos were approaching them.

"There appears to be a welcoming committee on the way," Inga called to the others.

"Uh-oh." Dori joined him in two slow bounds. "Welcoming? I doubt it."

The Mangaboos were beautiful, smooth-faced beings, dressed in fine, satiny robes trimmed with lace.

"They do not look angry," Inga said.

Dori shook her head. "They are vegetable people—they grow on bushes—and they don't have any hearts," she said. "So they'll look the same whether they invite you to admire their pretty glass city or decide to throw you into the Black Pit."

"The Black Pit?" Inga repeated, dismayed.

"It's a deep cavern inside those mountains over there." She waved behind them.

Rik snapped his fingers. "And that's where we want to be. The Nomes have tunnels everywhere, ones so old we've forgotten them. But some of them have to connect up to their pit."

"We can get to this Black Pit without being thrown into it, I trust," Inga said.

"The Mangaboos'll have to show us the way," Dori said.

This conversation took place while the doll-faced Mangaboos closed in around them. None of the Mangaboos spoke. They just stood there, staring. On some unspoken cue some of them pressed back, revealing a dainty young lady with a beautiful face and a star glowing on her forehead under curling dark hair.

This must be the princess that Dorothy had picked off the royal bush! Dori thought. She stared, remembered from her reading that the princess had begun her rule by walking on the air above everyone else, because she was royal, and then had calmly ordered Dorothy's animal friends thrown into the Black Pit.

"Who are you?" the Mangaboo princess asked.

"Visitors, your grace," Inga said, sweeping his hat off in a practiced bow. "Visitors to your fine land, on a royal

. . . *a dainty young lady with a beautiful face and a
star glowing on her forehead under curling dark hair.*

quest. We shall depart at once if your grace will be so kind as to furnish us with the directions we require to leave."

The princess stared at him. Her expression did not change, but Dorothy suspected she liked the way Inga talked. It was certainly very royal sounding.

Rik curled his lip. "Just a point of the royal thumb in the right direction will do," he said. He, too, was a prince, but his manners were not the least princely.

The princess ignored him. "A royal quest?" she repeated.

Inga bowed again. "I am Prince Inga of Pingaree."

Rik, not to be outdone, elbowed forward and pronounced in a loud voice, "And I am Prince Rikiki of the Nome kingdom."

The Mangaboo princess seemed to notice him at last. She turned then to Dori and said, "Are you a princess?"

"No—" Dori began, but before she could get any farther, the Mangaboo princess turned her back.

"Come. We will discuss your quest in my palace." She gestured to Inga and Rik, and began climbing up the air, her skirts held delicately at either side.

All the Mangaboos began climbing too, herding along the two boys. Dori was left alone on the glassy road, looking up toward a grand tower. The Mangaboos climbed and climbed, at last passing through an archway. Dori watched their distorted reflections until they became nothing more than winking dots of colored light; then she turned to explore.

She was just as happy not to be in the Mangaboos' company. Instead, she crossed a pretty little glass bridge into a garden full of flowers and ripe berries of all kinds. She picked and ate some dark, tart huckleberries and wandered through some trees toward what looked like a small lake.

She found a surprise. It was a lake, all right, but a transparent sheet of glass covered it. Dori stared down into the dark blue water below, fascinated by the glinting splashes of ruby, emerald, and diamond-bright silver made by the changing rays of the six lights in the sky.

"Help."

The voice was so faint she almost thought she'd imagined it. Was there a shadow, way down there in the water? Dori frowned and bent down with her knees resting on the glass over the edge of the lake. Yes! There were several shadows, all darting toward the other end of the lake.

"Please help!"

The voice was louder now, coming from the far side of the lake.

Dori jumped back onto the grass edging on the lake and hurried around to the far side. Below her feet the grass seemed to change color—pink, blue, and green again— before she reached the far side.

Dori emerged from a screen of leafy shrubs to a surprising sight. The glass cover had not completely closed in the lake after all. One shore had been left free. The glass around it was jagged, as if broken off. Suddenly the water along the shore slopped and splashed as if something just below the surface was struggling, and a moment later a figure surged up from under the edge of the glass, panting for breath.

It was a mermaid. Her long greenish hair streamed down and fanned out behind her in the water. She looked to be about Dori's age.

"Oh, thank you," the mermaid gasped. "Can you help us?"

Dori stepped down to the water's edge. "What's the matter?"

"That thing," the mermaid said, pointing at the glass. "We bring shells and rocks to try to break it, but they keep growing it back and we can't breathe! We can stay great lengths of time underwater, but every so often we must come up for air. Under glass there is no air. Merfolk who make the great journeys underground need occasional airing stops. This is one."

"That certainly doesn't seem like it would cause the Mangaboos a problem," Dori said. "Did you ask them if you could stop here?"

"We have asked many times. They either ignored us or threatened us. We've tried to be as quick as possible, but sometimes being quick means splashing." The mermaid grinned. "We do like a good splash. Especially the younger ones. They can't resist a little water on the Mangaboos' nice clean glass, though my mother told them not to, no matter how rude the Mangaboos are." She frowned. "But now they are sealing the lake, making it really dangerous for us."

Dori said, "I don't understand. Even if you splash, water dries. Why don't they want to allow you in their lake?"

The mermaid said bitterly, "They want the water to be still and smooth, no one in it, no unsightly ripples or splashes. Having a nice, neat glassed-in lake appeals to their sense of order. They hate everyone besides themselves, and they don't care if we run out of breath."

"Well, I care," Dori announced. "They are very selfish, that much I know."

The mermaid smiled. "Then help me break more of this glass. A big migration of merfolk is due any time, and they must be able to breathe. I promised my mother, Queen of the Freshwater Merfolk, that I would make certain their path is clear."

"I'll be happy to help. What we need is a big rock," Dori stated, and looked around the garden.

She spotted a fine piece of granite glittering in the changing light. It was about as big as an armchair. Ordinarily, of course, she couldn't budge such a thing, but the blue pearl in her shoe enabled her to easily heft the rock. With a gentle push, she launched it into the air. The boulder slid smoothly upward and then arced down, slow as a snowflake on a still winter's day.

Both she and the mermaid watched as it settled onto the glass about twenty feet from the edge. Cracks radiated out from under the boulder, and with an unmusical tinkle a great chunk of the glass broke off and dropped into the lake. The piece of granite fell in a moment later. *Floop!* Waves surged out in rings, dying down to ripples.

Dori and the mermaid princess looked at each other and laughed in triumph; then Dori started hunting for another rock.

Far above in their glass tower, several Mangaboos watched what was happening below. Their emotions—if you could say that such cold, unfeeling beings felt anything like emotions—were far from triumphant.

Inga and Rik were sitting with the Mangaboo princess in her audience room. The glass furniture was pretty, if you cared about pretty things. Inga was accustomed to them and Rik had no interest in how chairs looked as long as they were also comfortable. The princess's furnishings were quite uncomfortable.

Nor had the Mangaboo princess offered them anything to eat. Mangaboos didn't eat, and they didn't care if their visitors went hungry, since they didn't want visitors.

But still, royalty was royalty, and so the Mangaboo princess had been asking about the visitors' quest when one of her people glided sedately through an archway that opened right out into the air and said, "The girl is breaking the glass over the lake."

Rik was just saying, "And so I left the border of Oz, and traveled under the desert in one of my father's old tunnels, and—"

The princess turned her head. "I do not want the glass broken."

"She is not alone. Those disgustingly messy water folk are also breaking the glass."

"Then I must come at once," the princess said, and rose to her feet.

She stepped daintily out into the air, her skirts held just so, and with regal grace trod directly down through the air, over the tops of the garden trees, toward the lake.

Inga, who had been trained to remember his dignity when dealing with royalty, strode sedately after the princess, but Rik, who had no sense of dignity at all, scrambled down as fast as he could. He arrived first, with his legs and arms windmilling as he hit the ground.

Dori was just reaching for another good-sized rock when she felt a tap on the shoulder. Surprised, she looked up to see Rik jerking his thumb over his skinny shoulder. Dori glanced at the impressive party of Mangaboos descending as Rik said, "You're about to catch it hot!"

THE MANGABOO PRINCESS
stepped neatly onto the perfectly trimmed grass with her
smooth satin slipper, followed by Inga. She walked over to
where Rik and Dori stood by the lapping water.

In the water, the mer princess waited, looking worried.
Other young merfolk waited at a little distance, in water
that had been recently freed from under the choking glass,
listening with anxious faces.

"You must stop breaking my glass," the princess said to
Dori.

"Why?" Dori retorted, trying to sound as unconcerned
as the Mangaboo princess did.

"Because I will it so."

"I will the opposite," Dori stated, no longer even pretending to be polite.

The Mangaboo princess did not flush, or frown, or stamp her foot. She simply said, "This is my land, not yours. I do not want you here. I do want the glass covering the water, and I will have it so."

"Why?" Dori asked.

"Because we do not like the noise of those messy water people splashing about. We do not like the splashes, either. It makes marks on our nice glass."

"Water dries."

"We don't like it. We want a quiet lake to decorate our garden," the princess stated. "Water ought to lie still and smooth and neat. As quiet as glass."

"But the merfolk have to surface here. They need to get air before they journey on. They never stay; their princess here told me so."

"The needs of water folk are of no interest to us. We do not like them; we do not want them around. And if you interfere, we will throw you in the Black Pit."

"Oh, we'll be quite willing to go to the Black Pit," Dori said, "and you won't even have to throw us. We'll walk right in, if you'll just leave the lake alone."

"We will throw you in the pit whether you like it or not," the princess said in her maddeningly calm voice. "And the glass will stay over the lake. There is nothing you can do about it."

"Oh yes there is," Dori snapped back, her voice rising. "I know you people grow on bushes. I can pick another prince or princess off your royal bush. I'll pick one that will be nicer than you, and you will be out of a job."

The Mangaboo princess came as near to showing emotion as any Mangaboo ever did.

"I do not want to be out of a job," she said. "But even if I am, my successor will be just like me. She will not like nasty, messy intruders like you and those fish people there in the water."

Dori bit her lip. What now? she thought. What would Dorothy Gale do?

Inga had his hand in his pocket, and he was frowning as though listening to an unheard voice. He whispered to Dori, "These merfolk are cousins to our friends in the Nonestic Ocean. I have asked the white pearl for advice, and it says to remember Princess Ozma."

Ozma! Of course! That's just what Dorothy would do—not just remember Ozma, but make these Mangaboos remember her as well!

Dori gazed up at the ceiling of the cavern, far, far overhead. "You don't like people coming down here from the surface, do you? Well, I can promise you that if anything happens to the merfolk, Princess Ozma of Oz will send out great numbers of people to break your glass."

"We do not want any more of you."

"Too bad. Princess Ozma will send people to find out why you won't allow the merfolk in this lake, I can promise. Now, if you will leave the lake be, I will do my best to ask Princess Ozma, who is a very powerful ruler on the surface, to tell land people *not* to come here. She respects the wishes of fellow monarchs—if they are reasonable."

The Mangaboo princess looked at the lake. She looked up at the sky. She looked at her people.

The mer princess said, with great dignity, "As for us, if we are permitted to surface, we shall leave a special sign below to our people, requiring them to surface quietly, and not splash, but be directly on their way."

The Mangaboo princess said, "Very well."

Rik, meanwhile, had located a huge boulder. Beckoning to Inga, he bent to lift it.

The boys grunted and heaved. The boulder didn't budge.

"Step aside, boys," Dori said.

With one hand she bent down and lifted the big boulder. Then, while the Mangaboos stood and watched, Dori climbed into the air, balancing the great boulder on one hand. She stopped directly above the middle of the glassy expanse.

"Now," said Rik.

Dori nodded, took away her hand, and walked back down through the air as the boulder settled onto the glass with as much speed as anything in the Mangaboo land moved. *Click! Cra-a-a-a-ack!* Spiderwebs shot through the glass in all directions, quicker than lightning, and then, with a tinkle and a crash, the boulder broke through, shattering the entire glass cover into raft-sized shards. For a moment they floated on the water, like ice floes, and then gradually sank away.

The waters grew still.

The Mangaboos were still as well. One could say that they appeared thoughtful, as thoughtful as vegetable people ever are.

Rik crossed his arms. "And now, if you would lead us to your Black Pit, we will be on our way."

The Princess of the Mangaboos was a shade more polite as she said, "I do not understand you strange beings. Is it breathing that makes you so odd? Imagine wanting to go to the Black Pit. That is a terrible punishment for us."

Inga opened his mouth, but Rik said hastily, "Never mind that. Just point the way."

"One thing I do know," the Mangaboo princess said, looking at where the big boulder had once sat. "We wish to see the last of you."

As they started off, the mer princess waved Dori over.

"Thank you," she murmured, smiling. "You have done us a great service."

"Glad to," Dori said.

"If you ever need our help, please speak this magical charm three times:

'Bikido-mikido-zikido-zee
Bring the merfolk at once to me!'"

Dori repeated the charm, and the princess dove down, leaving no more splash than a couple of droplets. The others were moving away from the glass city as swiftly as

Mangaboos ever moved, and Dori hurried after them.

"Well, that was fun," Rik said after a time.

"What? Helping the merfolk?" Dori asked.

"No. Smashing all that glass. We don't make glass in the Nome caverns. Maybe we ought to, just so we can have the fun of smashing it."

Inga frowned in disapproval, but said nothing.

Dori eyed the Nome prince. "You mean you wouldn't have helped that mer princess?"

"No." Rik shrugged. Then he thought. "Well, maybe. I don't like these vegetable people. Don't like their glass furniture. It would have been fun to smash up that glass just to make them mad."

Inga said, "But as a prince, you must aid the merfolk because it is the right thing to do."

Rik snorted. "What's the right thing? It wasn't 'right' to these Mangaboos. To them, 'right' is keeping their city all nice without water spots."

Inga rolled his eyes upward. He was too polite to argue, but Dori wasn't. She frowned down at the soft grasses. "No, Rik. The Mangaboos were wrong. It would have been easy enough to ask the merfolk to keep the water still. Then everyone would get what they wanted. But they made it impossible for others to breathe just to make things look nice. That's wrong."

Inga nodded. "Beauty and order are fine things, but not if they endanger others."

"Eh!" Rik scoffed. "Danger is fun!"

Dori sighed. She did not want to lecture Rik on what he should think. It reminded her too much of Aunt Susan's lectures on how big girls "should" give up babyish things like imagination. "One good thing has resulted from our helping out," she said. "The mer princess offered to help me in turn."

"What can she do?" Rik jeered.

"I don't know about that, but I do know Ozma would be pleased."

"Ozma would be pleased," Rik mimicked. "Now you're not talking about right and wrong; you're talking about power. Whoever has the greatest power wins. Then they say that they were 'right' and the others 'wrong.' You did threaten to use Ozma's power against the Mangaboos."

Dori flushed. "It's not that way at all."

"Why not?"

"I didn't tell them she'd come conquering, but that she'd come if the merfolk were in danger. She told me herself she never interferes with other rulers, unless they endanger people."

"People should look out for themselves," Rik said. "A nice fight between those merfolk and the Mangaboos would be fun to watch—glass flying everywhere." He grinned.

Inga looked troubled, but said nothing. Neither did Dori.

Rik said, "So you admit that you used Ozma's power."

Dori crossed her arms. "All I know is, I will continue to help others if I can. Including you."

"Who says you have to? I can do just fine on my own," Rik retorted, walking on ahead.

"You were right to do what you did," Inga said. "Prince Rikiki is just angry."

"Why?"

Inga touched his pocket, and his expression closed off as he listened. Presently he said, "The white pearl explains that he is angry because Kaliko tricked him. I also think that he's angry because you lifted that huge boulder that we couldn't budge."

Dori sighed. "Well, he doesn't have to take it out on me. And I *like* helping others too," she added. "It's fun! So there."

THE MANGABOOS led them
to an unpleasant hill made of ugly green glass. The entrance
to the Black Pit was located halfway up a ragged, jagged
pathway full of shards and splinters. The Mangaboos, having accompanied the three adventurers without once speaking to them, turned around and marched sedately back down
the hill as soon as they had all reached the Black Pit.

The three entered cautiously. Walking required careful
steps. The cavern they were in was so vast that it even
included mountains, which rose in stages toward the cavern
wall and ceiling.

Rik led the way down into the pit. With his excellent
night vision, he did not find dark the least frightening. Inga
politely let Dori go next, and he fell in behind.

Dori remembered that after Dorothy, the Wizard, and

their other companions had come through, the Mangaboos had piled up stones to block the way out. What had happened? Landslide? Or did the stones magically vanish again, leaving a new entrance to the Black Pit?

Whatever the truth was, Dori was not going to find out now. She felt her way forward, guided by the sound of Rik's breathing. She thought to herself, I'm walking where Dorothy walked. Where is she? Has anyone found her yet?

"Here we go," Rik said presently. "I've found a tunnel."

After a long hike, Inga said, "I hope we will emerge on the surface again."

"If we do, I'll find a way right back down," Rik snapped. "Kaliko isn't getting rid of me that easily, the old villain."

"I hope Rik really knows his way around these tunnels. I don't want to get lost," Dori whispered to Inga.

Inga whispered back, "Well, if any one of us can find a tunnel leading to the Nome kingdom, it will be Rikiki."

"What's all the hissing and fussing?" Rik asked. "Secret plans?"

"Not at all," Inga replied politely.

"Of course," Dori retorted. "Secret plans to grab Kaliko's crown and keep it for ourselves."

To her surprise, Rik laughed. Then he said, "How did you get so strong? I wish I'd found a spell that did that. Was it Ozma?"

"It wasn't Ozma," Dori said.

"Huh."

Dori could almost feel Rik giving her one of his slanty,

considering looks. How she wished that she could see!

They all fell silent. The way had gotten steeper, and they needed all their breath for climbing. Even Dori. Super strength was great for lifting boulders and stopping the hammers of iron giants, but it didn't make a bit of difference when you were toiling and moiling straight uphill.

Up, and up, and up. Faint light filtered in from somewhere, just enough for them to see where they were going, but not enough to see color or detail. Dori began to feel very tired indeed, not to mention hungry. Those berries she'd picked in the Mangaboo garden were all she'd eaten since the picnic on the magic carpet.

Presently Rik gave a huge yawn, one the other two heard instead of saw, and he said, "I don't know about you, but I'm sick of this walking. I want to sit down and rest."

"A fine idea," Inga said.

Dori was too tired to speak. She sat down right where she was. The others did the same.

She felt around. The ground was silty in places, which was better than hard stone. She put her head down, meaning to just rest her eyes, and dropped off to sleep so fast she didn't even know she was dreaming.

Whirling lights and strange hissings and echoes filled her dreams with weird, nasty little monsters with snaky voices.

She was glad when Rik's voice broke into the unpleasant dreams. "Who's coming along?"

Dori sat up and rubbed her eyes. "I'm awake," she said.

"And I," came Inga's voice from somewhere ahead. "I couldn't really sleep, so I took the opportunity of scouting ahead a little, and I believe I spied a light not too much farther on."

"Well, then, let's find it," Rik exclaimed, running ahead.

Inga and Dori walked behind him more slowly. Inga looked somewhat tired in the faint bluish light. Thinking he might have had bad dreams too, Dori asked, "Why couldn't you sleep?"

"Because someone was spying on us in that tunnel," he replied.

"Spying?"

"Maybe worse. I think it might have been Nomes, but I couldn't see anything. I heard them, though. I figured that, since I have the pink pearl, all I had to do was touch the two of you and nothing could harm any of us. So I grabbed your shoe and the edge of Rik's tunic, and presently the noises went away. After that, since I was already awake, I decided to go exploring."

Dori realized that the whispery, slithery noises of those spies must have been the cause of her bad dreams. She shuddered.

"The white pearl told me to go this way, so I did. I figured that you'd be all right while I was gone, since you still have the blue pearl."

Dori nodded. "Thanks."

Inga said, a smile in his voice, "It was nothing."

Dori sighed. "If it weren't for Ozma counting on me, I think I'd just as soon go home. This isn't going the least like I expected, and, well, I just don't know how I'm supposed to help when Rik obviously doesn't want any help."

Inga waved a hand at the tunnel in front of them. "I believe Prince Rikiki might actually be glad of our help."

Dori snorted. The sound echoed, making her grin. There, if she could laugh, then things couldn't be so bad, even if she was tired, thirsty, hungry, dirty, and maybe lost. "Why do you think that?" she asked.

"If he truly did not want us, it would have been easy enough for him to abandon us and go on ahead. We'd never catch up in these underground caves."

"He may already have ditched us."

"Let's run and see, shall we?"

Dori nodded, and they both began to run, emerging into another tunnel that swiftly got wider, with light filtering in, painting the rough rock with blue shades and making bits of rock glitter. Around a great bend they found Rik waiting. His expression seemed odd to Dori, but behind him was the mouth of the tunnel, filled with light. The three ran the last few steps and surfaced into a lovely valley, closed in on all sides by mountains.

They stood there, squinting up at tall, leafy trees, some of them full of flowers, others bearing fruits of yellow, gold, crimson, and purple. Dori didn't recognize any of those fruits—the yellow ones were all the size of strawberries, the purple ones more like bananas, and the orange ones like plums—but one thing was certain: they all smelled good.

Her stomach growled. "Breakfast," she said, and ran down a little path to the nearest tree.

The others were not far behind. Each type was different: some sweet, some tart, some creamy, some crunchy, but all were very tasty. When they had eaten their fill, they each drank at a brook that splashed toward a wider stream.

"We've traveled upward, but not too far," Rik exclaimed with satisfaction. "We're not on the surface."

"What?" Inga asked, looking around. "It's light here, and the sky is blue."

"That's magic, not the sky above the surface," Rik said, pointing upward. "Do you see a sun?"

They all looked up. No sun up in the sky—and no shadows on the ground. The light, which was the lovely golden light of late afternoon, seemed to come from everywhere.

"So we are still underground. That means I can find tunnels," Rik announced with triumph. "That's what I'm going to do right now."

"May I accompany you?" Inga offered. "Two pairs of eyes might make the search quicker."

"Three pairs," Dori said. "We're here to help you, Rik. If you've forgotten."

Rik shrugged his bony shoulders. In his world, no one "helped" anyone, unless they planned on getting something back.

But here they were, all together, and it made sense for

three to search instead of one. So he said, "All right."

The boys started off at a rapid pace.

Dori followed more slowly. Suddenly she laughed, and up ahead both boys turned around.

"I think I might know where we are after all," she said.

The boys waited until she caught up.

"If that tunnel was the same that Dorothy and the Wizard were in, then this might be the Valley of Voe," she said. "Where the people are all invisible."

Just as she said the word "invisible," the trail ahead widened and then opened into a clearing. They saw a circular lawn dotted with flowers ranging from pale pink to pale blue. In the center of the lawn was a cottage, round in shape, with flowering vines growing up the walls.

They walked cautiously up to the windows and looked in. There was cozy furniture, all made of wood, with plump cushions on the chairs and cheery curtains on either side of the windows—but no inhabitants in view.

Rik frowned. "I don't like this at all," he said. "Invisible people have an unfair advantage. Let's get out of here. I know we're close—I just need to find another way home."

He turned around and ran back down the trail. Inga dashed after him, to keep him in sight.

Dori sighed as she pounded after them, wondering whether or not she should tell Rik about the magical Dama Fruit that made people invisible, when she heard a faint sound.

"Help!"

Then there was a great thrashing of bushes, followed by another, shriller call for "Hel-l-l-lp!"

The boys were too far away to hear. But Rik probably wouldn't come anyway. She knew how he felt about rescues.

"Oh! Please! Help!"

Dori raced past thick, dark-green leafy shrubs toward the shout and floundered to a stop when she saw a shape in the midst of a large, thorny bush.

Then she heard a growl.

"Gr-r-r-r-!"

A huge, fierce-looking bear was standing on the other side of the bush and swiping it with its claws. Dori jumped back.

"Help!" trilled the creature caught in the center of the thornbush.

Two more bears appeared, all three growling as they moved toward the thornbush.

Dori stared, aghast. Then she remembered the blue pearl. Bending down, she fixed both hands firmly at the base of the thornbush and yanked the entire thing free of the ground. Big globs of soil dropped from the roots as she waved the bush at the oncoming bears.

"Yip!"

"Yelp!"

"Yoop!"

The bears took one look at the little girl waving the bush and shambled off into the woods.

Dori bent and gently resettled the thornbush into its place, tapping down the roots back into the soil.

"That's good enough," a low voice grumbled. "Don't wake me up again."

A talking bush? Well, why not?

"I'm caught. I hurt," another, shriller voice whistled from the middle of the thornbush.

Pushing aside big waxy leaves, Dori reached carefully into the bush and discovered a bird there. Its neck was long, with rainbow colors glittering along it. The bird looked at Dori with one eye, then the other, and then the first again.

"Just a second," Dori said. "I'll have you out in no time."

"My plumage! It hurts. I'm stuck."

"Yes, I see," Dori said, pushing the leaves farther back. The bird had fantastically long tail feathers, all of which were caught by the thorns.

Grunting and pushing and pulling, she untangled the feathers. This despite the bird's frequent cries, "It hurts! Ow! Hurry! Oh! Bears!"

At last Dori freed the last of the feathers, though her arms were considerably scratched up. The bird leaped up onto her arm. It was surprisingly heavy, and Dori was glad she had the blue pearl.

"Thanks," the bird chirped. "You good. You help. I help you."

"It's all right," Dori said.

"No. I help. I must. Queen! Tasca Birds! Honor bound.

The bird leaped up onto her arm.

You go. I go. You save me. I save you. I must. Honor! Tasca honor!"

The squawks and chirps so close to Dori's ears were really shrill, and the way the bird's head darted around was hard to look at.

Dori smiled, setting the bird on the branch of a nearby fruit tree. "There you go. It's all right. Go ahead and return to wherever you live. How did you get caught, anyway?"

"Tivi berries! Love them."

Dori peered into the very center of the thornbush, and sure enough, she spotted clusters of pale lavender berries.

"Yes, I see them. Can't you eat anything else?"

"Yes. Love these. Best berries. I'm queen. Have best!" The Tasca Bird then shrilled a high, piercing note.

The whirring of wings caused Dori to look up. Five smaller birds, all with trailing tail feathers, alighted on various branches, tweeting and squawking. They were all about the size of the Tasca Bird, but none of them had nearly so long a tail.

"Girl! Saved me. We serve," cried the queen in her ear-tingling shriek.

"We serve!" the other birds shrilled back.

Dori groaned. "It's all right! I don't need saving."

"We must." The Tasca queen flapped her wings in agitation. "We must!"

"Must! Must! Must!"

"All right, all right," Dori said soothingly. "Come along, then." She wondered what Rik was going to say when he saw all these noisy birds, and winced. She hoped by the time they reached the Nome kingdom, the birds would decide that maybe their honor would be satisfied with her hearty thanks.

D ORI LOOKED AROUND.
She was alone—except for the Tasca queen still sitting on
the fruit tree branch and her five companions overhead.
The Tasca queen's feathers had become all tangled again.

Dori sighed, reached down, and carefully disentangled
the long streaming feathers while the Tasca queen shrilled
in alarm.

"I have to go," Dori said, and started backing away.

The Tasca queen started flapping her wings to take off,
but to no avail. She flapped so hard her beak opened and
faint squeaks came out. Without thinking, Dori lunged
forward, gently slid her hands under the bird's stiff feet,
and shoved her into the sky. Once she was in the air, her
grand tail feathers floated out and the Tasca Bird could fly.

With the Tasca Birds flying above her, Dori launched herself back down the trail in search of the boys.

The pathway stayed narrow, overshadowed by the ferny trees and shrubs—all of which she was getting thoroughly sick of seeing. From somewhere ahead she heard distant birds chirping, and leaves rustling in the breeze, but no sound of Rik or Inga. "Boys! Where are you?"

"We help! We seek!" With a whisper of wings, three of the Tasca queen's court took off in different directions over the treetops.

Dori kept walking, on the lookout for bears.

Presently the birds came flying back. "Here! Here! Here!" they all cried, and they arrowed away in one direction.

Dori plunged after. The Tasca queen, making a great effort, circled around and then flapped away behind them, her tail feathers streaming.

Dori ran until she stopped short at a surprising sight: Rik sitting on the ground, rubbing his head. "Ouch," he protested.

Inga stood off at the side, trying hard not to laugh.

With her noisy escort flying around overhead chirping shrilly, "There he is! He's there! He found! We found!" Dori walked over to the boys. "What happened?"

"I don't rightly know. He started running. I was behind, trying to keep up, we rounded that great purple bush there, and suddenly he went splat! As if he'd run into a wall. Then he fell."

"I hit something," Rik snapped.

"Yes. Me, you clumsy thunk. That hurts!"

"Who?"

"Me!" came a voice from the middle of the clearing. "Why don't you watch where you're going?"

Rik scrambled to his feet and put his fists on his hips. "How can I watch what I can't see?" he demanded.

"Oh yes. I forgot. I'm so used to it, you see. Being invisible, I mean. We almost never run, because we don't want to smack into each other. But I just couldn't help it, it was such a nice day."

"It's not polite to run," said a new voice, a very prissy one.

"That's my big sister," said the first voice.

Dori just knew the older sister was a teenager, the kind she hated the most: the bossy kind who is always right.

"And if my little sister had not been running, she would not have bumped into someone," the prissy voice declared smugly.

"Sorry," the younger voice mumbled.

Rik shrugged. "I'm all right. But why are you all invisible?"

"So the bears won't get us," the prissy one said as though it was obvious.

Rik scrambled to his feet, and then said in the direction of the younger voice, "Do you happen to know of any tunnels around? Besides that one in the mountain back that way, that leads down to the Mangaboo lands?"

"Oh yes, there are caves and tunnels all over," the younger voice said eagerly. "We play in them a lot."

"Just point me in the right direction," Rik said.

"There."

No one moved.

"Um, I think I'd better take you," the invisible girl said, realizing that no one, including she herself, could see her pointing finger.

A small hand took Rik's, tugging briefly.

They all started off down the pathway.

"Voro," cried the prissy voice. "You come back this instant."

"No," Voro replied promptly, stopping.

Dori knew she'd stopped because Rik stopped—but not before *she* ran into a solid, small girl shape.

"Oof!"

"Sorry," Voro said contritely.

"Sorry," Dori said at the same time.

Voro turned around. They could tell because of the direction of her voice. "I knocked that boy down, Vuru, so the least I can do is show him the way out of our valley."

"Mother will be quite angry with you when I tell her."

"Go right ahead, tattletale. And I'll tell Mother about how you've been hunting Tasca feathers, just to put in your stupid hair that no one can see anyway."

"I like the way they feel," Vuru said. And they heard a stamping and rustling noise, the sort of noise you hear when someone flounces away.

"Hah!" the Tasca queen screeched overhead. "Dropped feathers! Gone! Now know where."

"Who is that? And why do we have these birds flapping around our heads?" Rik asked, jerking his thumb up over his shoulder. "I wish *they* were invisible," he added.

The Tasca flock squawked in protest. The queen ignored Rik with lofty disdain, sailing from tree to tree with her beautiful feathers trailing.

"I saved her from a thornbush," Dori admitted. "Where a bear was about to get her. I think she's joined us. In gratitude."

Rik smacked his hands up over his face.

"The one there with the great long feathers is the queen of the Tasca Birds," Dori added in a somewhat sulky tone. "And I guess the other ones are her court of honor. She says she has to stay with me until she can save my life, as I did hers."

"Oh, great," Rik snarled. "Just what we need. A lot of noisy birds when we'll need to be really quiet."

"I can't help it," Dori snapped right back. "She means well."

"Tasca Birds are very rare," Voro said. Everyone had forgotten about her. "Very beautiful, too."

"Yes," the queen chirped, high above them, her rainbow-colored tail streaming out behind her. "We are. Most pretty birds!"

"And the *queen*, too," Voro added. "I wish I'd been the one to save her."

"Me too," Rik said, giving Dori a disgusted look.

"Maybe next time" was all Dori could think to say.

"Well, come along. The closest tunnel is this way." Voro tugged Rik's hand. "Follow me!"

Rik struck out in front.

Dori fell in step beside Inga. "Whew," she said in an undertone. "It seems to me that every time I turn around, there's more royalty. You two boys—Ozma, of course— two mermaid princesses, and now this bird. If Voro turns out to be a princess—"

"I'm not," called a cheery voice from up ahead.

"I didn't know you could hear me," Dori said, not quite willing to point out that she'd meant her conversation to be private.

Only how could you be private around invisible people?

It seemed to Dori that, pretty as this Valley of Voe was, she'd be glad to get out of it.

"Well, you're more interesting than this skinny boy with the sour face," Voro said. "Anyway, we don't have any princesses in Voe. Princes, either."

Inga said, "Once King Rinkitink told me that when he was younger, traveling the lands north of the Nonestic Ocean, he came across the Kingdom of Galimoph, where everyone was related to the royal family, because it was such a small place. So everyone except one single family were all princes and princesses."

"Did they all live in castles?" Dori asked.

"No, they moved the ordinary family into the royal

palace, to keep them safe and sound. And all the princes and princesses wait on them hand and foot to keep them happy and contented, since they are so special."

"What do the princes and princesses do when they aren't foot-and-hand waiting?" Voro asked.

"Why, they milk the cows, bake the bread, feed the chickens, and tend the vegetable gardens," Inga said. "After all, someone has to!"

Dori laughed, thinking: I wonder what Em would say if she visited that place? Homesickness filled her at the thought of her sister. I hope Em is doing all right, Dori thought, and she walked a little faster, as if that could get her home to Kansas just a bit sooner.

10

HERE'S THE CAVE
I was telling you about," Voro said at last. "One of our
favorite places to play."

They had emerged from the forest before a rocky cliff
with a dark passage near its base.

Light slanted in from cracks overhead as they walked
through the opening into a cave that smelled of dust and
mold and something else, something a little weird.

"We have to be careful because of the Hizzers," Voro
said. "That's why our parents don't like us searching for
pretty stones in the caves, or playing hide-and-find there."

"Hizzers?" Dori asked.

"Snake people."

Rik said, "They live way underground. They really hate
Nomes," he added. "Nomes aren't a tasty meal."

"They keep saying that they want to taste us children from Voe," Voro said. "But first we have to become visible. They don't want to eat us while we are invisible, because they might become invisible too, and they think they're far too beautiful not to be seen."

"As if you'd want to become visible," Dori stated. "Just to be eaten!"

"Well, Mom says they aren't the smartest, but they make up for it in being mean. Anyway, we run away if we hear them hissing and sliding around, but the strange thing is, after they go, we always find pretty stones on the floor. Like these."

Rik, Inga, and Dori watched as a small, glittering red stone rose up into the air.

"That's just an old flawed ruby," Rik scoffed. "Nobody would want that."

Voro said in a small voice, "Well, I think it's very pretty. And it will look even prettier out in the light of our Valley of Voe."

"Huh," Rik said. But it was not the "huh" of disbelief, it was the "huh" of discovery. It was an important discovery, but for the moment he kept it to himself.

"I think it's pretty too," Dori said, examining the stone. It glittered with crimson, scarlet, and deep, deep red lights.

"I put the really pretty ones on the windowsill in my room," Voro said. "I'll add this one. I wonder how they got here."

"I cannot imagine," Inga said. "I know so little about life underground."

"I don't know either," Dori said.

"Boys! Chase!" The Tasca Bird shrilled, flapping around in circles overhead.

Rik said in a loud voice, "Where do you find the most of these stones?"

"Oh, in the tunnels down that way," Voro said, taking Dori's hand and pointing it. "I never go in that far. It's too dark, and very scary."

"Good idea to stay away," Rik said, nodding. "The Hizzers aren't the worst of what's down there."

Dori was immediately suspicious. There was something in the way he said "Good idea to stay away" so quickly. Why did he suddenly care?

Because he's hiding something, she thought.

"Well, here's where I said I'd take you, so I think I'll go home now," Voro said.

"Thanks!" Dori exclaimed, and Inga echoed her.

"Good idea," Rik said, nodding. "Very good idea."

He then bent down, with his hands on his knees, and examined a gray stone. Dori and Inga watched him, wondering what he was looking for. It just seemed like an ordinary stone to them.

After a while Dori said, "Is that a magic stone, or something? We could help, if we knew what to look for."

"I was waiting until that girl went away," Rik said. "I mean, how do you ever know when someone invisible is really gone, or standing around listening to hear what you say when you think they're gone? It's what I'd do," he added cheerfully.

"I think you frightened her away with your talk of worse creatures than these mysterious Hizzers," Inga said. "She's gone."

"Well, there *are* worse creatures," Rik stated. "Much worse. There are the Dinods. Huge reptiles with great teeth, and they love eating animals. People best of all. But the powerful mages like Glinda the Good and Ozma of Oz won't let them make snacks of people, and animals are too smart to venture down into their dark, smelly caves, so they are forced to eat vegetables. It makes them very, very nasty."

"They sound horrible!" Dori exclaimed.

"And meaner than the Dinods and the Hizzers together are the Spider-Bats."

"Bad! Very bad!" the Tasca queen trilled.

"Bad! Bad! Bad!" shrilled her court, flying around in circles overhead.

"And the worst of all are the Phanfasms. But I think I recognize these old tunnels, and if I'm right, I ought to find some friends down that way, if they've managed to escape from their boring duties," Rik said. Then he gave them a derisive smile. "If you still want to come along, that's where I'm going next."

Dori thought of the blue pearl in her shoe, and the pink pearl in Inga's pocket, and shrugged. "We can handle any

There are the Dinods. Huge reptiles with
great teeth . . .

Hizzers or Whizzers or anything else that comes our way," she said.

"Yes, and I wish I knew how," Rik said. "Because you sure didn't have all that strength when we tangled with that witch."

"Let us depart," Inga suggested, sensing an argument.

"I'm ready," Dori said.

Rik plunged down the middle of the dark tunnel, leaving the other two to follow as best they could. Dori had stumbled about ten steps when a tiny light darted out of the darkness and dropped into her hand.

"You see!" cried one of the Tasca Bird's court.

"Thanks," Dori said, holding up the glowing stone.

It gave off just enough light so that she could see the rough, rocky ground ahead. Inga, who had been feeling his way, paused and waited for her to catch up. Rik, who could see in the dark, was far ahead.

With the help of the light, and the birds flying overhead, Dori and Inga made much better speed.

They had almost caught up with Rik when they heard something . . . voices high and mocking. Some kind of nasty creature?

"Hey!" Rik yelled.

The voices stopped.

"Hey, Tiki! Tavi!" Rik cried. "I'm back!"

11

FOR A SHORT TIME, all Dori could hear was the mournful drip of water somewhere. Then the whirring sound of wings flapped overhead, and the Tasca queen alighted on her shoulder with a thump.

"Nomes! Inside!" the queen cried.

"Nomes!" her court chirped in unison. The sound echoed down through the tunnels: *Nomes, Nomes, Omes, Om!*

Then the sound of pattering feet echoed from one of the tunnels, and the cave was soon filled with spindly Nome boys with flyaway hair and round, gray faces.

"Riki!" they cried.

"Tiki! Tavi! Jubjub! Jabi! Wok!" Rik cried back.

"Where have you been?" one of then asked. Then he

peered at Inga, Dori, and all the Tasca Birds. "And what are these?"

Rik waved at two of the boys. "Here's my cousins, Tiki and Tavi. And those are my friends." He indicated the rest. "That's Inga. Came along for some reason. And as for her—"

"I'm Dori," she stated quickly, before Rik could say something that would make her mad.

"And she's strong enough to throw a Hizzer back into its lava pit," Rik added.

Tiki and Tavi whistled.

"Sounds almost as mean as my sister," said Tavi as he backed away.

"It's been so boring since you left," Jubjub said to Rik, ignoring Dori and Inga. "We just do all the things you invented, over and over. Are you back to stay?"

"Yes." Rik stuck his fists on his skinny hips. "I want my kingdom."

The boys all started laughing and hooting. Jubjub actually rolled on the ground.

Rik just stood there until the noise had died down a little, then said, "And I'm going to get it back."

Tiki jabbed a long, skinny thumb in Rik's direction, his bulgy eyes even bulgier. "He's *serious*."

"Why?" Jubjub asked.

Tavi rubbed his eyes. "How?"

"Haven't decided yet," Rik said. "But I do know one thing. Either you help me, or else when I do get the crown, you'll all be tossed down to the Dinods."

"What's in it for us?" Wok asked. He was the smallest and skinniest, with a voice almost as high as a Tasca Bird's.

"You will not have to work; you can play all day and throw real jewels at the Hizzers instead of old rocks that the girls throw away."

Tavi laughed. "So that's how you found us? Did you find our throwing rocks? We found where the girls toss the ones they think too ugly to make into jewels."

"Sure did." Rik shrugged. "I remembered we used to play around in those old tunnels a long time ago. When that area was forbidden, of course."

"Of course," Tiki exclaimed, grinning. Then he winced and rubbed his head. "Then that one tunnel collapsed, just like they said."

"So we came over here and started chasing Hizzers and throwing the old rocks at them," Jabi said.

"Found the rocks clear out to the mouth of the cave," Rik said. "I just knew that mess had to be from you lot."

His friends grinned.

"Some of those rocks we threw at the bears. Keep 'em from wanting to take over our caves," Jabi said.

"Bears are too surly. Not much fun," Wok piped up.

"It's been really boring since you left," Jabi admitted. "Even getting into trouble is boring."

"Well, you're about to become dukes—as soon as I'm king," Rik said, waving a hand grandly.

"As long as being a duke means no work," Jabi said dubiously.

"Of course not!" Rik exclaimed, indignant. "What's the use of being a duke if you have to grub in the mines or chip stones? You get to swagger about handing out orders to groveling minions and not lift a finger, except to throw things if the minions are not fast enough."

"Groveling minions," Jabi exclaimed. "I remember those from the bad old days with your dad, before he lost his memory!"

"Who are the groveling minions?" Wok asked, rubbing his knobby head.

Rik threw his hands wide. "Everyone else!"

"I think they've forgotten how to grovel," Wok said, frowning in perplexity.

Jabi muttered to Jubjub, "Can't fancy my dad being a groveling anything," but if Rik heard, he paid no attention.

Tavi very much liked the notion of no work. "Then what are we waiting for? Let's go!" he yelled.

"What's the plan?" Tiki said, walking backward. "You know Kaliko isn't going to just up and hand you the crown, now that he's got it sized to his head and comfortable."

"Oh, we'll think of something," Rik promised. "First, something to eat. Then a place to plan. Where are you hiding these days?"

"We'll show you!" Wok shrilled. He danced along ahead of them, waving his sticklike arms. "This way! This way!"

He led the way down the dark tunnels. Dori carried her light-stone, and the Tasca Birds, who were silent now, took off and flew along overhead. Or rather the court took off.

The queen strained to lift herself, flapping hard, until Dori gave the bird a mighty push. Then the queen drifted along behind her court.

They walked down and down, the tunnels getting narrower and rockier and nastier. Dori tripped three times, and Inga twice.

But just when Dori felt she could bear the dark no longer, the tunnel led into a much wider one, lit with grayish light. The floors were smooth, and the rock overhead glittered with bits of emerald, diamond, ruby, tourmaline, tiger's-eye. The air this far down below was not as hot, or stuffy, as Dori had feared. It smelled musty, but not bad.

They passed through a cavern with many stalactites and stalagmites, then over a narrow rock archway. Water rushed below in the darkness, heard but unseen.

At last they reached a cave made cozy by brightly striped blankets on the floor.

"Here's our new hideout," Tavi said proudly. "Not a grown-up yet has found it." He turned. "Jubjub and Jabi, your turn to go find us some food!"

Jubjub grumbled and Jabi made a face, but they departed willingly enough.

As everyone else settled down, Dori whispered to Wok, "Where are the Nome girls?"

Wok's gray eyes went round with surprise. "Probably down either making stones into jewels, or else fighting Spider-Bats for fun," he whispered back. "You don't want to meet any, believe me. *We* don't want to meet any. They hate humans, and they're much meaner than we are."

"Oh." Dori remembered what Tavi had said about his sister, and decided not to pursue the subject.

"So what's the news in low places?" Rik asked.

Tavi shrugged. "Not much. Kaliko throws the crown at Klik's head. Just like your father used to do."

"I ought to be good at crown throwing," Rik predicted with confidence. "I've shied so many stones at Dinods trying to chase us."

"Remember the time we found those Phanfasms trying to sneak over the Great River?"

Rik laughed heartily. "Oh yes! I think I beaned twenty of them before they snuck back to their side of the rocks." He grimaced. "Those were nice diamonds, too. And they took 'em when they went!"

"Oh, when you're king, you can have as many as you like. Us, too. We can play Battle Bones all day, and we won't have to do any mining first to find them." Tavi chortled.

Tiki said, "The more I think about it, the more I like the idea of you being king."

"So what's the plan?" Jubjub asked, coming in followed by Jabi, each with a laden tray.

"Something with plenty of laughs for us," Wok advised.

"Of course," Rik exclaimed, looking surprised. "Otherwise, why bother?"

Jubjub and Jabi set down their trays.

Rik rubbed his hands as he surveyed what they'd brought.

Dori and Inga looked dubiously at the trays. The gold and silver plates were all gem encrusted, with gems far finer even than those owned by Inga's parents. But the food on the plates was pretty much all gray in color, except for some round things that were dark brown. Unappetizing, to say the least.

"Hmm," Rik murmured, licking his lips. "Sozzle stew, gimble glue, and crunchberries. It all looks good. Help yourselves," he invited, waving a hand at Inga and Dori. "Gotta keep that strength up." He grinned. "We might need it."

"May I ask what sozzle stew is?" Inga asked politely.

"It's pretty much all mushrooms of various sorts," Wok said. "We grow 'em special. For when we can't get grub from the surface."

Dori sighed. She wasn't particularly fond of mushrooms, but she was hungry, so she tried a bit off of each plate. It was all surprisingly good, especially the brown berries, which tasted a lot like chocolate buttercreams, only crunchy. She ate heartily.

Afterward the Nome boys sat back and reminisced about tricks and jokes they'd played on one another, on the Nome adults, and especially on some of their dangerous underground neighbors. Then, one by one, they all fell asleep.

Dori and Inga were both tired. Used to judging their day by the sun rising and setting, they had no idea what time it might be. They were just relieved when they heard the others start snoring. Now they could get some rest too.

Dori stretched out on a blanket, feeling the blue pearl's comforting presence with her big toe, and decided she'd just sleep with her shoes on.

Down in the royal caverns, three figures peered around the great gem-studded door to the royal throne room.

"Your majesty?" Klik called, nervously fingering the gold chain around his neck.

"Yes?" Kaliko replied quietly.

Klik backed away. The other two—the Long-Eared Hearer and the Lookout—promptly pushed him forward again.

"Go on," whispered the Long-Eared Hearer. "You have to talk to him."

"You're the grand chamberlain," the Lookout added. "That means he has to see you first."

"But—"

The two spies prodded him so hard he stumbled into the throne room. Klik promptly fell to his knees and covered his face with his hands.

Nothing happened. He gradually peeped up between his fingers and saw Kaliko lounging on the throne, lazily twirling his great golden crown around on his thumb.

"Your Majesty," Klik began.

"Yes?" Kaliko's voice had gotten, if possible, even more quiet.

Klik scrunched down into a ball and covered his face again. Again nothing happened. He looked up, puzzled. Of late, when Kaliko got angry, he'd taken up the long-respected royal custom of heaving everything in sight at the chamberlain. And his aim was getting better.

Klik got it out fast: "Rikikifoundhiswayback." Then he ducked down again, this time with his arms over his head.

Nothing happened.

"Withtheprinceandthelittlegirl."

Still no reaction.

Emboldened, the Long-Eared Hearer stepped in, taking care to keep Klik's plump form between him and the monarch. "I heard him just a while ago."

"They somehow escaped the Hizzers you sent to the great tunnel. I saw them emerge safely into the Valley of Voe," said the Lookout, peeping over the Long-Eared Hearer's shoulder.

"And I heard him afterward," said the Long-Eared Hearer. "He somehow found where his foolish band of brats has been playing, up in the old forbidden passages where the Hizzers and the Dinods like to roam."

"And none of those tiresome brats has been carried off yet?" Kaliko asked, sighing.

Klik looked surprised. "Uh, no." He slowly rose from the floor.

"And here I went to all the trouble of forbidding them to go there! Of course they'd go there first thing, and so I hoped to get rid of them. The Hizzers must be getting slow and lazy."

The Lookout edged in, still keeping the Long-Eared Hearer and Klik between himself and King Kaliko. "I saw them," he said. "I saw them stealing food. Then they went to sleep, in a new hideout."

The Long-Eared Hearer, losing his fear of flying objects from the kingly fingers, added slyly, "And I heard something about practicing throwing the royal crown at you." Which wasn't what Rik had said, but after all, spies are spies.

"And I saw them gathering. They are armed and ready to march on us, soon's they wake up," the Lookout added, not saying that the "arms" were the flawed stones they carried to ward off roaming Hizzers.

Despite what he'd told his minions, Kaliko had not cast a spell sending Rik, Inga, and Dori down the wrong tunnel to Mangaboo land expecting them to stay away. He'd sent them away so he could gain time in which to think. He'd had his time. And now he was ready for them.

He smiled.

The three counselors, watching anxiously for signs of royal anger, saw that big smile with all those gleaming teeth, and their skinny knees started knocking.

"Let them come," Kaliko said, smiling even wider. "I have a new plan. A far, far better plan."

Ow!"

"Ooch!"

"Hey!"

Dori woke up to the cries of protest. Inga was already awake beside her, smiling with amusement. She sat up in her nest of blankets and saw Nome boys rubbing their heads or arms and scowling.

Rik stood on the other side of the cave. As Dori watched, he lobbed pebbles at each of the other round, blanket-covered lumps.

Boink! Bink! Boonk!

"Ow! What'd you do that for?" Tavi complained.

"I'm practicing being king, of course," Rik explained, tossing another stone up and down on his palm. "Now, who else wants to keep sleeping on the job?"

Most of the Nome boys sat up, rubbing their knobby gray heads underneath their wispy hair. Before they could speak, the Tasca queen's court flew in, each bird bearing something in its beak.

Nomes waved their arms irritably, trying to scare away the birds.

"Hey!" Wok piped up in his high voice. "Why are they in here? Birds don't belong in the Nome kingdom!"

The Tasca queen flew by, turning her head from one side to the other, saying, "Dori! Eat!"

Bunches of grapes and seed pouches plopped into Dori's lap, and the birds sailed upward, roosting on knobs of rock just under the ceiling, where they ate their own breakfast of seeds and nuts.

Dori held them up. "You shared yesterday, so it's only fair I share now. Who wants some?"

"Phoo!" Jubjub held his nose.

"Blugh!" Jabi turned away, pruning his face.

"Paugh! Fresh fruit? How disgusting," Tiki exclaimed.

"Only if we're starving," Rik explained. "And I was starving long enough in Oz. Not a good mushroom anywhere. So who's going to bring *me* breakfast?"

"Get it yourself," Jabi snarled, as Dori divided the fruit with Inga and they began eating.

Rik glared at the Nomes. "I see I have to get in some good crown-throwing practice," he threatened.

"Hey," Jabi fired right back. "You said we'd have a lot of fun if you were king. Waiting on you hand and foot isn't fun at all."

Rik shrugged. "Someone has to do it, until I get the crown from Kaliko."

"I'd rather go back to the mines."

"Then we'll put Klik to work doing the boring things like getting breakfast. But first I have to get that crown. Let's go," Rik said, rubbing his hands.

"What's the plan?" Tiki asked.

"Easy. Easy." Rik waved a hand. "See, Dori there has the strength of twenty. She'll pick up Kaliko and hold him over one of the fire pits until he agrees to my demands."

"I won't," Dori said.

"What?" All the Nomes turned her way.

She crossed her arms. "I won't hold anyone over a fire pit. And you can't make me," she added, "since I do have the strength of twenty. So think up another plan."

"Well if you won't help, why are you here?" Rik grumped.

Good question, Dori thought. "Oh, I'll find a way to help," she said. "But not that way."

Rik shrugged. "So we do it the hard way, then. You lot have to get all the boys down in the mines to march on the king and boot him out. Tell them we get to play, and the grown-ups do all the work."

The Nome boys saw nothing wrong with either Rik's reasoning or his plan. "Hurray!" they cried.

"What about breakfast?" Jubjub put in, rubbing his fat, round belly.

Rik waved a hand. "That can wait until we take over the royal caverns. The food in Kaliko's kitchens has always been the best in the entire kingdom."

The boys had no objection to this, and raced out. Dori

heard their voices echo back from high and low, whooping with triumph. Rik walked after them.

Dori and Inga were left alone with the Tasca Birds, who were busy preening their feathers after their breakfast of seeds.

"Well, that doesn't sound good," Dori muttered. "It sounds to me like they're doing just what Ozma was afraid they would do, starting a war. Only it's not Nomes against other people, it's Nome kids against the grown-ups!"

Inga nodded once, and then frowned. Dori stayed quiet. She knew by now that when he frowned that way he was listening to the white pearl.

Inga looked up. "The white pearl tells us to wait."

"All right, then," Dori said, shrugging. She popped the last grape into her mouth, then wiped her hands on her shorts. "I'm not so sure I trust any of these Nomes! But we may as well follow them and see what happens."

Inga had no objection to make. He stood up, brushed his fine clothes, resettled his cap on his head, and waved most politely for Dori to go first.

The Tasca Birds launched into the air, all except the queen. This time Inga, with a courteous "Allow me," launched her up.

At last she gained enough altitude to soar right over-head. Dori, looking up, said, "Those tail feathers of yours make it so difficult for you to fly."

"Feathers queenly," the bird shrilled. "Pretty! Witch gift!"

"You mean you weren't born with them?"

"No! Looked same. Dull! Want beauty! Wish from Witch."

Dori stared in amazement. She wasn't going to say anything out loud, but wow. That bird was vain!

I guess it's not just humans who do stupid things to themselves just for looks, she thought. Shaking her head, she ran after the others.

She'd just caught up with the boys when a loud, rhythmic sound echoed up from far below. They emerged onto a catwalk of stone that arched over a vast cavern. Dozens of other bridges and walkways both above and below them ran between tunnels built into the great granite cliff faces. Far, far down the low hiss of rushing water echoed up the rock walls from the unseen cavern floor.

Rik stopped in the middle of the catwalk to gaze downward.

"Uh-oh," he said. Then, turning to Dori, with a grin of challenge he added, "I might be needing that strength of yours."

Thud, thud, thud! Pounding feet struck the stone like drums, as hordes and hordes of Nomes appeared from every tunnel, each wearing armor of glittering silver worked with stones, and each carrying a spear or sword of polished, gleaming bronze.

Trum, trum! The Nome soldiers marched out onto the causeways, then stopped, looking up in silence.

Rik crossed his arms. "Well?"

A round, fat Nome emerged from the forces below. He

A round, fat Nome emerged from the forces below.

had a great golden chain of beaten medallions draped around his shoulders.

The solemnity of the moment was slightly marred for Dori when she noticed Wok squeezing out from between two of the other boys. He wiggled his fingers at the armed Nomes below, and whispered, "Hi, Dad."

"Hey, son," one of the Nome soldiers whispered out of the side of his mouth.

Klik cleared his throat. "His Majesty, King Kaliko, requests Prince Rikiki, son of Roquat, also known as Ruggedo, to come before him in the royal throne room for a royal palaver," he proclaimed in a loud voice.

Rik waited until the echoes died away, then he said, "And what's all this?" He pointed at the armed Nomes.

"An honor guard, of course," Klik said politely. Then he added, "To make sure you get there."

Rik shrugged. "Why not? Was on my way to see Kaliko anyway. Tiki! Tavi! If something happens, you know what to do."

"Right! Right!" they answered as the Nome boys closed ranks behind their leader.

Dori and Inga fell in behind Rik too. The children sauntered quite bravely out in front of the huge mass of silent, armed Nomes. The Nome army parted to let Rik and his companions by, then closed in behind them, every Nome stamping his tough bare feet in unison. The sound echoed through the cave just like drums.

In silence—except for the drumming feet—they marched up and down tunnels, across bridges, and through caves with smooth walls decorated with brilliant gem-stones. Dori looked around in wonder. The Nome kingdom was actually quite beautiful, in a weird way, once you got used to there being no sunlight or green things growing.

The caverns got bigger and grander, until at last they entered the largest of all. Carvings and gems glittered from every surface. At the far end of the chamber was a golden throne on which sat a short, round Nome with curling brows.

A golden crown rested on his head, a lovely golden crown set with spectacular gems of every color. The crown looked to Inga and Dori just a trifle battered on the sides. King Kaliko smiled broadly.

"Here you are at last," he said to Rik.

Rik stared back, unsure of what would happen next. He did his best to look defiant, the way a Nome prince ought to.

Kaliko stood up, pulled off the golden crown, and tossed it to Rik, who caught it. The Nome prince gazed down in astonishment at his father's crown.

"Ruling," Kaliko said, "is far too much work. I've been so bored. It's time to retire and enjoy the fortune I've amassed." He waved his hand toward the throne. "All yours, my boy. Have fun!"

And he sauntered out of the throne room.

The Nome army marched out after the ex-king, the echo of their stamping feet dying away, leaving the new ruler alone with his friends—and Klik the chamberlain.

R IK LET OUT a long sigh.

He grinned, dashed up, and threw himself on the throne, hooking one raggedy leg over the carved chair arm.

Then he set the crown on his head. Being too large, it promptly sank down over one ear.

"What's your first command?" Tavi asked, racing up to the throne.

"Oh, make it a good one," Jubjub crowed, jumping up and down.

"Breakfast, of course. A mighty feast!"

All the Nome boys turned to Klik. "We want the best dishes in the kingdom," Jabi ordered.

Rik waved a lazy hand. "And you may as well get some surface food as well, for those two." The royal finger indicated Inga and Dori.

"It shall be done instantly," Klik said, bowing.

And it was. The royal cooks must have been fixing a fine feast for Kaliko, for in no time at all a procession of Nomes marched into the adjacent dining room and set down great silver platters, each studded with rubies, emeralds, and diamonds of rare shades of blue, yellow, and pink. Off came the lids, and delicious aromas rose, smiting them all.

In addition to plump stuffed mushrooms, there were tiny ones in fine sauces, chopped and fried and broiled and baked ones of all hues, as well as many vegetables, cheeses, and fruit pies. Apparently Kaliko had a taste for the foods of the surface, just as a change of pace.

"Let's eat!" Rik cried, racing in.

The Nomes stampeded, leaving Dori and Inga to follow. Everyone found a great carved chair, struggled to pull it back, and sat down. For a short time the only noise was that of Nome boys diving at the various serving platters, grabbing fistfuls of food.

"Hey! Leave some for me!"

"Get off that platter so a person can reach!"

"Outta the way! Outta the way!"

When they'd piled their favorite foods high on the beautiful porcelain plates (and these, too, were edged with fine gemstones), the noise subsided to gobbling, crunching, lip smacking, and gulping.

Inga and Dori, who had waited politely for their turns, stared in dismay at the wreckage. Dori felt her appetite shrivel up when she saw the fingerprints in the mashed potatoes, the broken and scattered bits of the pie, and the steamed vegetables all scattered down the table.

Jabi turned to say something to Tiki, but his mouth was so full of food that no one could understand him, and he sprayed bits all over Tiki's sleeve.

"Hey!" Tiki protested, flicking the bits back in Jabi's direction.

"Hah!" Jabi whooped while, unnoticed, Wok swiped one of his crunchy cheese balls.

Dori pressed her lips together. Inga, sitting beside her, looked sorrowful. He was far too well mannered to say anything impolite, especially at the first banquet of a new monarch. Dori had no such qualms, but she wasn't sure what to say.

Then a figure appeared at her side. "Would you care to sample these?" It was Klik.

He held out a platter of celery stalks with something in them that looked like cream cheese.

"This sort of food is repulsive to most Nomes, but our former king had a taste for the exotic."

Dori and Inga helped themselves. Nodding their thanks, they began to eat.

After a time the Nome boys were done. Dori and Inga finished their meal of celery with some fruit that the Nome boys had left untouched. Then Rik got up and ran back into the throne room.

"Mine! Mine! Mine," he yelled, jumping onto the throne. "Ouch." He winced, jumping up again and rubbing his bony backside. "Gotta watch out for those stupid rubies."

He sat down more carefully, ignoring the snickers, snorts, and hoots of the Nome boys, who had been quite entertained by the way their king had shot into the air.

"Do it again," Wok crowed.

"Never mind that," Rik said. "Now what?"

"Fun, of course," Tiki cried.

"You promised us fun!" Jubjub yelled.

"We're dukes, remember?" Tavi bellowed.

"What are we dukes *of*?" Jabi asked.

"Who cares? As long as everybody else has to bow to us!" Wok piped. "That means I don't have to be last anymore, just because I'm smallest."

Jabi said, "I'd rather play first."

"We can play Battle Bones," Rik began.

"But we can do that any time," Jubjub protested.

Klik came forward, smiling. "If I may advise Your Most Royal Majesty?"

Dori frowned. Klik's smile was broad; his eyes crinkled. But it was not a smile of friendliness.

"What is it, Klik?" Rik asked, leaning his elbow on the throne.

"Well, Your Majesty must now make protection of the kingdom a first concern. Since Kaliko is no longer king, the magic of the kingdom is yours."

"Magic!" Rik exclaimed. "Now, that sounds like fun. What kind of magic?"

"Well, you have to learn it," Klik said. "Like your

father did, and Kaliko as well."

"You mean even though I'm king, I still have to do lessons?" Rik protested.

"Well, yes. If you wish to protect the kingdom, and make use of your magical aids."

Rik sighed. "I guess you fellows might as well go play a game of Battle Bones, then. Tell everyone you're now dukes," he added as his friends ran out. "That means everybody has to bow to you." And to Klik, "Bring on the magic lessons."

Klik glanced toward Dori and Inga, hesitated, and pulled out a golden whistle. He tooted three sweet notes. The Tasca Birds swarmed overhead, repeating the notes and adding more chirps. Klik and Rik ignored them, but Dori smothered a laugh.

Two Nomes wheeled in a great cart, full of fat, musty books. They parked the cart next to the throne, bowed, and scampered away.

Rik took the first book off the pile and opened it to the first page. "What is this boring stuff?" he said, then read from the book. "'Ye beginning wizard must forthwith learn ye basics. Ye first basic magic word is 'bo.'"

"You can't make spells until you learn the basics," Klik explained.

Rik groaned. "All right. I guess I'd better get started."

"May we help?" Dori asked.

Rik opened his mouth as if to say yes, but Klik said smoothly, "Alas, no, but a very kind offer, young lady. Nome magic must remain the secret of the Nomes."

"Yes. Nome secrets. Very important," Rik said.

"If I might suggest you come this way, perhaps we can find something to entertain you while His Royal Majesty is busy with his lessons." Klik smiled and bowed so low his golden chain clattered and clunked.

Dori gazed at him doubtfully. She didn't like his smile, but he spoke so politely, and he had brought them something to eat, when Rik and his friends had paid no attention.

"All right," she said in a slow voice. "Inga?"

"We are here to help," Inga said. He doffed his cap and said, "Lead on."

Klik did. They followed him out of the throne room, leaving Rik whispering behind them, "Bo, bee, boo, bop, bing, bubu."

Klik led Dori and Inga down several lofty hallways, carved with fantastic shapes and studded with gems, to a spacious chamber filled with lovely furnishings.

Inga paused on the threshold, his expression doubtful. "A moment, please," he said to Klik. "I believe I have been here once before. And I do not believe I wish to be here now."

For answer Klik raised his golden whistle and tooted once.

Dori and Inga heard a stampede of Nome feet on the rocky floor, and a moment later they were ringed by Nomes, all carrying spears, some of polished bronze, others of hammered gold. All the spears had nasty, sharp points.

"Please," Klik said, bowing very low. "Inside, most honored guests."

One of the Nomes prodded Dori. She glared, ready to grab that spear and twist it into a pretzel, but Inga caught her eye, then shook his head slightly.

Dori realized he did not want to risk having the Nomes find out about the pearls, so she followed him inside the guest chamber. The Tasca Birds flew in overhead and perched on the splendid furnishings that lined the rocky room.

"Very kind of you, I'm sure," Klik said, still with that false civility. "And now I may go attend our new king."

The rocky door slid into place, shutting them in.

Dori sighed. "What now?"

"I have been here before," Inga said as he walked slowly around the room, studying the walls.

Dori almost said, "I know this room too, from an Oz book," but decided against it. She still wasn't sure if she should tell Inga that she knew all about his adventures from a book. After all, he didn't seem to know that the Royal Historian of Oz had included his adventures in the *Accounts of Oz.*

"I think we're safe to use the pearls to escape—"

Inga hadn't even had time to finish his sentence before the rock door slid open again and admitted two peculiar figures.

They were skinny, knobby-looking Nomes, one with very bright eyes that seemed to look in all directions, the other with rather long pointy ears.

Dori stared. "The Long-Eared Hearer," she whispered.

"Yes," said he, smiling a nasty smile. "And I heard you talking about your magical pearls. All three of them: white, pink, and blue. Hand them over."

Dori turned to Inga, and he stared at her aghast.

"And I see them too," the Lookout said, in an even nastier voice. "There's a little bump in that funny-looking shoe of yours, and as for him, I see two bumps in his pocket." The Lookout pointed first at Dori's feet and then at Inga's fine velvet tunic.

Inga stepped close to Dori and drew himself up, standing very like a prince. "If you know about the pearls, then you know you cannot harm us." He took hold of Dori's arm. "And if you try to take them, she will pick you up and throw you back out that door."

"Who's first?" Dori asked, rubbing her hands.

"If you don't surrender those pearls at once, I'll call the guards to spear those birds you have sitting around, and we'll serve them up for supper," the Lookout said.

Squawk! Shriek! The birds shrilled in protest—as well they might.

Dori almost clapped her hands over her ears.

"And next, we'll go find someone for the bears to eat, like maybe those invisible children up in Voe, where I first heard you come back into our tunnels," the Long-Eared Hearer added. "No pearls protect them!"

"Now," the Lookout commanded. "Or that bird with the long tail gets it first."

The Tasca queen, alarmed, struggled to fly up into the

air, but the Long-Eared Hearer was far too fast. He caught hold of her tail feathers and she squawked in protest, then sank down onto a diamond-studded armchair.

"Here," Dori said in haste, kicking off her shoe.

The pearl bounced out, rattling across the stone floor to where the Lookout bent to pick it up.

Inga reluctantly slid his hands into his pocket and withdrew the other two pearls. In silence he handed the pink one to the Long-Eared Hearer, who chuckled in triumph.

The two spies headed out the door with the Lookout muttering, "Now, I want that pink pearl. You can have the blue."

The Long-Eared Hearer retorted, "No, the pink one is mine!" The Tasca Birds fluttered out the door over the heads of the spies as they bickered.

The rock door closed on the Lookout saying, "If you want the pink one, you have to take this white one. It's gabbling stupid things in my ear. . . ."

Inga sank down onto a gold-stitched hassock. "I'm sorry," he said to Dori.

"Well, I don't see that it was anyone's fault. They heard us talking, is all."

"I know," Inga said, polite as ever. "But I am sorry about what I fear will happen next—"

And right then a door slid open on the opposite side of the chamber.

"Uh-oh," Dori exclaimed.

"UH-OH!" SAID EM, watching her sister in the snow globe. "Dori! You'd better—"

The phone rang.

"Argh!" Em carefully set the snow globe on her desk and ran downstairs to where she'd left the phone. "Why don't I ever remember to take it with me?" she said out loud. She talked out loud a lot now, just as she always had the TV going downstairs. It made the house seem less lonely.

Em thudded down the stairs and skidded into the kitchen. There lay the phone where she'd put it the night before, on the table. "Hello?"

"Hello, Emma, dear." It was Mrs. Gupta from next door.

Em eased over to the kitchen window and stared out

through the steadily falling snow. She could barely see the outline of Mrs. Gupta's house, but even so, she felt like ducking.

"Snowing hard, isn't it?" Em said, trying to make conversation.

"It certainly is! Quite a storm. But we can be thankful that it isn't too bad here. Now, how are you girls? Are you all right?"

Em heard that tone of voice: she knew Mrs. Gupta meant, *Are you sure you girls aren't getting into trouble?*

"Oh, we're fine," Em said, scouring her brain for the most boring things she could think of. "I just finished the dishes." (That much was true, at least.) "Dori is up taking a bath."

"A bath! That child must be the cleanest girl in Kansas!"

Em made a hideous face, remembering that both times Mrs. Gupta had come over, she'd said that Dori was in the bathtub.

"Well, she washes her hair a lot. Long hair, you know," Em babbled, longing to hang up and get back to the snow globe. What was going on? How did those two nasty Nomes manage to make Inga and Dori give up the pearls? If only she could hear the voices as well as see!

"Oh well, I guess, as long as your mother doesn't mind a big water bill. It sounds like you girls are perfectly all right. It's snowing so hard I have to admit that tramping across seems a real hike."

Em realized that Mrs. Gupta was making a joke, and she forced out a giggle. It sounded fake to her ears. "Today is not a day for hikes," she said, hoping she sounded more normal.

"I must say, your house seems nice and quiet, so you can't be getting into too much trouble!"

Another joke. Em giggled again. Her hand squeezed the phone, wishing the power lines would go down. No! Then Mrs. Gupta might come over and insist on staying!

"Your mom will be calling in the next couple hours, and I want to be able to give her a good report."

Em tried to think of the most boring activities she could. "We're going to fix some spaghetti. When Dori gets out of the bath, I mean. Then clean the kitchen. And then read. We're reading up a storm," Em added desperately, thinking, Or at least I am! "We get extra reading points at school, you know. Would you like me to tell you about the extra reading program? Or I could tell you all about our 'vacation math challenge.'" Now that would be good and boring!

And it worked. Mrs. Gupta said somewhat hastily, "That's all right, Emma. Your parents will be so glad you girls are working hard. Tell your father to give me a call when he gets there, all right?"

Dad!

Em hung up, smacking her forehead. She'd forgotten all about Dad coming home. How to solve that? Em clunked the phone down on the table again and groaned as she pounded up the stairs to get the snow globe.

Ring!

Clatterty-clatter! Back down the stairs. "Hello?"

"Hey Em-girl."

"Dad!" She looked around wildly, hoping he wasn't on his cell phone right outside the front door.

"Say, kiddo, I've been calling the airport. It's completely shut down. I'm trying to figure out what to do next, since flapping my arms doesn't seem to get me into the air."

Em giggled weakly. "We're fine, Dad."

"Oh! Well, then, in that case, I guess there isn't an emergency."

"No! Go ahead and stay there, Dad. We're fine, I promise!"

"I promised your mom to be there by tonight or tomorrow. But the weather and the airport don't seem to want me to keep my promise."

"Oh, everything is perfectly fine! Mrs. Gupta's always checking on us—she practically lives here."

"All right. Here, let me speak to Dori."

"Oh! She's"—Em stopped, thinking: How many times did I tell Dad she was in the bath?—"down in the basement folding laundry, and I'm upstairs. In the bathroom," she added quickly.

"Well, then, give her kisses and hugs from me, and I'll see you girls as soon as this mess gets cleared up, all right?"

"Sure, Dad! Bye!"

Phew! Em sighed with relief as she set the phone down.

Then she started back up the stairs, paused, looked back. "Oh no you don't," she muttered, and tromped back down to get the phone.

"You're not going to ring at me as soon as I get that snow globe," she said to the phone, glaring at it.

When she got to her room, she sighed again. "Talking to a phone!" She dropped it on her desk and then turned to the school picture of Dori she'd set on her chest of drawers. "This lying business really stinks. How could anyone like it?" she said, glaring at her sister's smiling face. "I'll bet I've used up an entire lifetime supply of lies."

Ring!

"Hi, dear."

"Hi, Mom!"

"Is your father there yet?"

Here goes another one, Em thought, making a face. "I think he's on the way. The phone had a lot of crackle in it, so it was kind of hard to hear."

"He did call?"

"Oh yes! Just five minutes ago!" That much, at least, was true.

"Oh good, then he didn't forget. I was afraid he'd forget. Now, let me talk to Dori. I always seem to get you! I don't want your sister feeling left out."

How many baths has she taken for Mom? "She's out taking a walk."

"A walk! In this weather? I just talked to Mrs. Gupta, and she said it's snowing blankets!"

"Oh well, it's not quite so bad. Right now. And so Dori just wanted to go to the corner. To get some air."

"Well, I can understand that," Mom said. "I'm feeling shut in myself. But I'm glad to say Gran is feeling much better, now that the fever is gone."

"Give Gran kisses and hugs for us, okay?" Em said.

"Yes, I will, but don't hang up. Let's chat until Dori gets back. As I said, I feel a tad shut in too, and I miss you girls."

"And we miss you, too!" Em said, hopping up and down. What now? What now? "I just didn't want to miss a special program, on the science channel. And you know how Dori dawdles along, because she's always looking at trees, or thinking about adventures!"

Mom laughed. "Well, it sounds like you girls are busy and having a good time, and that's the important thing. I'll talk to you later." She hung up.

Em put the phone down and this time collapsed backward onto her bed, thinking wearily that Dori might be facing Nomes and bears and those nasty Mangaboos, but somehow they didn't seem as tough as all these well-meaning grown-ups on the phone.

Em sat up.

"Nomes?" She raced to her desk and got the snow globe.

She shook it up, shut her eyes, and said clearly, "Princess Ozma, I wish to see what Dori is doing." When she opened her eyes, there was Dori!

Dori and Inga were feeling their way slowly along in what looked like a dark tunnel. Em crouched down, staring. "Uh-oh. Watch out, Dori," she muttered to her far-away sister. "Remember those falling handcuffs. . . ."

DORI AND INGA cautiously entered a grim, rocky corridor, lit just enough for them to see great jagged rocks.

Inga sighed. "Your pardon," he said. "I fear I was mistaken in suggesting we not resist." He sat down onto a rock and put his head into his hands. Dori barely heard his muffled voice, low and unhappy. "I have lost the pearls."

"We both got ourselves into this mess," Dori responded, as overhead there was a rustling noise. "Attacking them would not have been any better. I think they would have carried out their threats against the birds."

The Tasca Birds couldn't really be seen in the dimness, but Dori heard chirps of effort and then the sound of all of them flapping away, including the queen.

Good. She hoped they would reach a safe place—and stay there.

Inga said with regret, "King Kaliko used the same trick on me before, closing me into these rooms," Inga said. "But with the pearls and my memory of what happened, I thought we could get safely out of them. I did not foresee those threats."

Dori frowned. "Here's what I think. I think Kaliko might not know about what Klik did to us. You notice he went away. It was Klik who brought us here, and of course those two spies got the pearls. I'll bet it was all their plan."

"Unless Klik acted on the orders of the king. Former king, I should say." Inga corrected himself.

"Former?" Dori snorted. "He gave up way too easy. I think he's up to some trick. And Klik knows what the trick is, but has plans of his own."

"That does sound plausible," Inga admitted. "Though it seems uncivil to malign a fellow member of the royalty."

Dori clamped her lips closed. She wanted to say "Royalty, shmoyalty, bad kings are worse than bad citizens," but she suspected that that might not be civil, either. And Inga was always so well mannered.

She sighed to herself, wishing that Em was with her.

Kansas seems farther away than ever just now, Dori thought. Aloud she said, "We need to get out of here."

Inga sat up straight. "Yes. You are right. If we do not have the pearls, then we must rely on our wits. My father would tell me it's good training for a prince."

"Good training for anybody," Dori said, trying for humor.

Inga attempted a smile. It wasn't very convincing, but Dori liked him all the better for it just the same. "Well, then," he said. "We'll get out of this place and then find a way to recover the pearls."

"Good plan," Dori said firmly.

One thing at a time, Mom always said. Dori whispered the phrase to herself as she and Inga walked on. The light in the cave they were in was dim, but the archway they were approaching gave onto a cave with no light at all.

They walked forward slowly, and gloom closed in around them.

Meanwhile, the Tasca Birds flew through the caves until they found an old tunnel too narrow even for Nomes.

As soon as they found light and a place to perch, the Tasca queen chirped to her court, "Pearls! Find!"

"Pearls!" chirped the court. "Pearls! Find!"

"Soft," the Tasca queen ordered. "Quiet! Two-legs do not look up."

"Quiet! Quiet!" the five birds cheeped softly.

"Go! Find! Listen! Return here," the queen commanded.

*As soon as they found light and a place to perch, the
Tasca queen chirped to her court, "Pearls! Find!"*

The five birds took off in five different directions, flying swift and silent through the dark tunnels and caves.

B ack in the dark cave, Dori and Inga shuffled to a stop. Inga said, "I remember this. There are several corridors that lead to a circular chamber."

"The one with the steel door," Dori said, forgetting to hide the fact she knew about these wicked traps. "Let's feel our way along the walls, and don't put your hands out in front of you!"

Inga was surprised at her mention of the steel door. But he decided now was not the time to ask.

They parted, each staying close to a rough, cold, rocky wall. A sudden whirring noise startled them both, but they clapped their hands to their sides. A moment later they heard a clatter. Then a second clatter.

"Handcuffs!" Inga said, kicking at one with the toe of his velvet shoe. "Just as I expected. Indeed, I know where we are." He looked over in the direction of Dori's voice. "So you knew about the steel door and the magical handcuffs, then?"

"Yes."

"Yet neither of us has the pearls," Inga marveled. "So you cannot be hearing the white one's good advice. May I inquire how you knew these things?"

"I read about it," Dori said as she felt about on the stone floor. "The Royal Historian of Oz wrote about it. Quick! We have to find that steel door before it closes. I bet you anything the handcuffs trigger it."

Inga said, "Here's the steel door. We do not dare step through, lest the door slam onto us."

"So we find a big stone. That shouldn't be hard in this rocky mess of a cave," Dori responded.

"True," Inga replied. "But what, may I ask, is 'to trigger'?"

Dori said, "Ah! Look what I found. A nice big stone, but it's heavy. Help me push it into the doorway."

Inga felt his way over, and together he and Dori shifted a big block of granite, rolling it awkwardly toward the steel door. They wedged it in the doorway, then Dori straightened up, wiping her hands on her shorts. "As for triggering, it means to start something happening. Triggers belong to a kind of weapon. Never mind—I don't think you have them in Pingaree. Oooh! Here it comes."

Both she and Inga paused, waiting, as the steel door closed on the stone with a *whang!*

They hopped over the stone through the crack between the edge of the steel door and the rocky opening.

"Okay, next threat," Dori whispered.

"A much bigger threat," Inga said.

"Right. Isn't this the chamber with the giant?" Dori returned. "We can't wrestle any magical giants, not without those pearls!"

"I have a better idea," Inga said. He searched the cave floor for a moment, then held out something. "Get a stone like this, one that feels glassy."

Dori dropped to her knees and scooted along, her fingers searching over the rubble on the floor. At last she found one, and just in time.

Thud! A powerful foot stomped down, making the floor tremble slightly. *Thud!* A second step. The magical Giant who guarded the next chamber had been summoned up by their presence, and now it was coming for them.

"I hope you don't expect me to throw this stone," Dori muttered, her heart racing. "I have rotten aim."

"No—just do what I do," Inga whispered back.

He took a sturdy stance as the footsteps stomped nearer, each one louder than before. Stones rattled and jumped on the floor as the giant approached, and then Inga and Dori saw two glowing red eyes appear in the darkness.

"Now," Inga said, raising his stone.

Dori watched him angle the stone's glassy side; a reflection of the nearest glowing eye flickered over the rough walls of the chamber. Of course!

Dori yanked her own stone up and caught the light from the right eye just as Inga reflected the fires of the left eye back into itself.

"Argh!" the Giant yowled, clapping its hands over its eyes. It lurched sideways and slammed into a rock jutting out of the wall. "Ow!" It pulled its hands away, and again Inga and Dori used their crystals to confuse and blind the

Giant. Howling and growling, the Giant stumbled off to the side, blinded and confused, and the two slipped past, completely unnoticed. They heard the stone door roll closed behind them.

"All right," Dori said, slightly breathless. "Next is the fake floor, right? The one that drops out from under you?"

"Yes," Inga said.

"I have an idea. Just follow me."

Inga nodded, then realized she couldn't really see his nod. So he said, "Very well, then."

Together they felt their way through the misshapen archway to the next chamber, an enormous cavern that smelled of running water.

"Hold it!" Dori called.

She stepped just far enough in to feel stone beneath her feet. Then she jumped back into the safety of the archway.

Dori dropped to her knees, and Inga leaned over her, both of them peering down into the dimly lit cavern. The floor slowly began to sink, vanishing more rapidly. With a great whoosh of cold, wet air, the stone dropped down and sent up a mighty splash from the rushing river below.

"Now we can climb down," Inga said. "That was a good idea."

With care, they climbed down until they stood on the edge of the black, rushing water of the river. Dori knelt and stuck a finger into the water. Brrrr! It was ice cold.

She looked up. Inga was only a dim shape standing nearby. "I fear there are no stones large enough to form a bridge," he murmured. "And we don't have the strength to lift them even if there were."

"I think I have another idea. I hope. I mean, I hope it works," Dori said, still kneeling. She faced the water, cupped her hands around her mouth, and sang out:

"Bikido-mikido-zikido-zee
Bring the merfolk at once to me!"

Nothing happened. Dori wondered if her voice could be heard above the thunder and rush of the river.

Raising her voice, she called:

"Bikido-mikido-zikido-zee
Bring the merfolk at once to me!"

And then, for the last time,

"Bikido-mikido-zikido-zee
Bring the merfolk at once to me!"

Then, with several little splashes, heads popped up in the water all around Dori! Her eyes had gotten used enough to the darkness to make out the smiling face of the mer princess.

"Hullo!" the princess cried. "We were just about to play hide-and-seek with the dolphins. Heigh-ho, I didn't think you would call so soon!"

"I'm sorry to disturb the game," Dori said. "But we're trapped here, and cannot get across."

"Oh, we can carry you," the mer princess said with a cheery laugh. "It will be great fun! Are you playing a game?"

Dori grinned. "We are not playing a game. Some of the Nomes tricked us, forcing us into their magical chambers. Up there"—she pointed way up the rocky chasm, to where a cliff could just be made out in the dreary, dim light—"is the only way out, a final chamber covered with nasty burning coals."

"Ugh." The mer princess made a face. "We do not like fire. But we can help you with water magic. Nothing easier," the princess proclaimed. "Here. Let me fetch my sisters. The spell I'm thinking of is a big one, and will require all of us to perform."

With a little splash, she dove back down. Dori and Inga saw the light gleam on her silvery scales. Then, with a graceful twitch of her tail, she was gone.

"That was quick thinking," Inga said.

"Well, it's also my last idea," Dori replied with a nervous laugh. "Next good idea has to be yours."

Inga nodded gravely. "The first thing we must do when we escape these chambers is to locate those two spies who took the pearls."

Splash! The mer princess appeared a moment later, surrounded by mermaids who looked more or less like her.

"You do not mind getting wet?" the mer princess asked.

Dori turned to Inga, who said, "A good dousing would be refreshing."

"I need a bath anyway," Dori said to the mer princess. "Thanks a lot!"

The mer princess gave Dori a merry smile, and then the mermaids formed a big circle and began weaving their fingers through the air, singing softly. A blue-silver glowing line stitched through the air from one mermaid's hands to another's. Round and round the glowing thread darted, faster and faster, the singing turning into a kind of low hum.

A kind of silvery doughnut appeared in the air within the mermaids' circle and the water beneath slowly churned, round and round, rising into a funnel.

One moment Dori and Inga saw silver fishes swimming in the funnel, playfully flitting, and then *sploosh!* A cold, shocking wave of water hit them.

Next thing they knew they were spinning around the top of the funnel, gasping and paddling desperately in order to stay afloat. Then the funnel rose over the cliff and spilled, in a great stream, right through the archway into the next chamber.

Fazoom! Steam fizzled and sizzled up around Dori and Inga in towering clouds as the water carried them safely over the glowing coals.

Then the water funnel receded, vanishing back into the river.

A girl's voice echoed up from below: "Are you all right?"

Inga and Dori cried together, "Yes! Thank you!"

"It was fun!" came the last cry, and the sound of splashings as the mermaids dove below to resume their games.

Dori and Inga stood there shivering. "Maybe we should dry off before we do anything else," Dori said through chattering teeth.

Inga could only nod. In the stronger light, they could see each other's blue lips. That river water, unwarmed by any sun, had felt like melted snow.

Dori edged as close to the chamber of glowing rocks as she could, and at once felt their radiating heat. She held out her arms and closed her eyes as warm air bathed her face.

When her front felt toasty and warm, she turned around to dry her back, and looked Inga's way. He was busily brushing off his splendid clothes, making them look fresh and neat.

Dori glanced down at her rumpled summer clothes and snickered. "Well, at least I'm clean as well as dry," she muttered. And who cared about a few wrinkles? Maybe not being royal helped!

When they were completely dry, Dori looked at Inga and said, "Well, we did it!"

Inga bowed, grinning. "I have to say, it was rather fun." His grin faded to a look of worry. "But now it is most urgent we recover the pearls."

"And we can't ask Rik to help us, can we?" Dori asked. At Inga's decisive shake of the head, she said, "I agree. I like Rik, as far as one can like a Nome, but I think those pearls might be far too much temptation."

Inga nodded. "I do not trust Kaliko, not at all. I believe you are right that he gave in far too easily. That suggests he has a cunning plan."

Dori sighed. "Well, then, that's two big jobs: getting the pearls back, and figuring out what Kaliko is up to. I just wish we knew what's up with Rik while we were stuck in here."

Inga bowed, gesturing toward one of the tunnels. He was smiling. "I think I may know what Rik has been doing," he said. "Let us proceed."

16

DORI AND INGA emerged into the main corridor, which was still silent, dimly lit, and smelling of old, musty rock.

"Here is the door to the furnished room," Inga said. "I remember that much."

"And down that way are the handcuffs and the Giant and all the rest of the traps." Dori pointed at the dark chamber, then made a face. "I sure don't want to do that again!" She sighed. "So what do we do? Just sit here until someone remembers us?"

Inga nodded, looking around for a clue to any other way out. At last he sat down on the ground with his back to a portion of rock less rough than the rest.

Dori shut her eyes and also slid down the wall to the rocky floor. "All I know is, I'm hungry."

Inga turned her way. "I do not know how long we were in those chambers—it could very well have been hours—but I suspect we aren't forgotten, and thus will be let out before too long."

Dori sighed. "You mean by Klik and his two nasty helpers?"

"No." He smiled again. "I was thinking of Prince Rikiki."

Dori sat up straight, hope returning. "What do you mean?"

Inga's smile turned into a grin.

"I mean that while we were facing all those traps, Prince Rikiki was facing, for the first time, all the trappings of kingship. If I do not miss my guess, he will be missing us any time now."

Rik was in his new throne room, his lap full of big, heavy, and very dusty books of magic.

While Inga and Dori were feeling their way slowly down that first long, dark hallway, Rik had tried to study. Now, everyone knows that you can't just do complicated things without practice, but Rik had been escaping from his teachers for so long that he'd completely forgotten what studying was.

He frowned at the first page of a particularly dusty

tome. It listed some basic words in magic, ones he would need in order to build magical spells. Once again he obediently tried to repeat them, beginning with "bo" . . . and soon he stopped.

"These don't make any sense," he muttered.

Right underneath the list, in big fancy letters, it said:

The Nomish Wizard Must Commit These Words to Memory!

All right. Magic was useful, and might even be fun, Rik thought. At least, it would be fun to turn old Klik into a toad if he got too pushy.

So he started again, this time on the second list. He was tired of the first list. "Biki, booki, binki, bobidi . . . bunk!"

That last word wasn't in the list. Rik realized that by the time he'd gotten to "bobidi" he had already forgotten "binki."

So he started over. He read the words, shut his eyes, recited the first three . . . and forgot "bobidi."

"I hate this!" he yelled.

He skipped down to the bottom of the page and saw, in even bigger, more threatening letters:

DO NOT READ ON UNTIL YOU HAVE MAS- TERED THE BASIC "B"'S!

Rik slammed the book closed. "I'll do it tomorrow," he muttered, and tossed the books off his lap.

Dust rose. Rik glowered at the pile of books. He thought of all those pages and pages to be memorized, and he was still stuck on the first page of the first book!

"I know," he said, snapping his fingers. "I'll hire a wizard who can put learning magic into a pill, and I'll swallow the pill. Instant mage!"

Having decided that, he reached for the bell cord hanging by the throne in order to summon the chamberlain, then decided he didn't really want to see Klik. But what else to do?

While Rik was looking around for something fun to while away the time, Klik had arrived at last at the end of many long, curving, old tunnels. He almost took a wrong turn at a new rockslide, but at last reached the room where he had told his two spies to meet him. He paused just outside the door to catch his breath. Inside, he could hear the two arguing.

"No, I want the pink pearl."

"No, I want it. You can have the blue one."

"I want the pink."

"Me!"

"No, me! Listen, Lookout—"

"I hate listening," the Lookout said sulkily. "You look here."

"I always listen," said the Long-Eared Hearer. "And right before you started bellowing, I heard Klik coming. What if he demands all the pearls?"

"No. Let him have that stupid white one."

Klik grinned. His spies were the best in the entire kingdom at watching and hearing, but not at thinking. Just the way he wanted it.

"Let Klik have what?" he asked, sauntering into the chamber. The other two jumped guiltily. "Give those pearls here. I need to get back in case that brat Rikiki wants to order me around some more. If I am not there, and he goes looking, Kaliko will get suspicious."

The Lookout exchanged glances with the Long-Eared Hearer. "You can have this one. Then we'll each have one. Fair is fair."

Puzzled, Klik held out his hand and took the white pearl the Lookout handed him. He realized he was hearing whispering, and looked around the chamber.

"It's the pearl," the Lookout said, just as Klik realized the whispering was inside his head.

You must restore me and my mates, the pink pearl and the blue pearl, to Prince Inga.

"No," Klik said, holding the pearl between thumb and forefinger and shaking it.

The pearl just repeated itself.

"What is this?" he asked, annoyed.

The Long-Eared Hearer, who could hear the whispering even though he didn't have the pearl, scowled. "Good advice."

Klik snorted in disgust. "I'll throw this thing down the nearest chasm!" But when he moved to a long crack at the far end of the chamber, the pearl whispered, *If I am destroyed, the other pearls will lose their powers.*

Klik glared at the two spies. "Give those pearls to me," he commanded.

"No," the Lookout said triumphantly.

"No," echoed the Long-Eared Hearer. "And you can't touch us, either. One of these pearls gives you super strength, and the other protects you from harm."

Klik sighed. "All right, we can figure it out later. Before we can act on our plans, we have to find Kaliko. I know he's lurking somewhere, spying on Rik, but I don't know where. We have to get him safely out of the way before we can deal with Rikiki. Speaking of whom, it is time for part two of Kaliko's plans for *him.* I have to go. Meet me at my room for dinner, and you'd better have news!"

He scurried away.

Rik strolled slowly around the quiet throne room. Here he was, king at last. He sat on the wondrously carved throne with all its fabulous jewels, but if he wasn't careful, they poked him in awful places. He could look up at all the fantastic carvings of strange and frightening beasts, but they didn't scare him. He'd seen them too many times in his life. It was far more fun to watch visitors cringing at them. And all the glittering gems, some of them bigger than his fists? Who cared? He realized he was bored. Not just bored, but lonely.

Where was Dori, and that natty prince fellow he'd found so irritating? Now he'd be glad of their company. He thought sourly, They've probably run off to play Battle Bones, just like my new dukes.

He yanked off his crown. At least he could get in some crown-throwing practice. That was a very important part of Nome kingship, and fun, too.

He slung the crown at a big emerald on the opposite wall. It bounced off the wall with a ringing *tink!* and rolled and bumped along the floor.

Hmm. No one to fetch it for him. Klik was gone some-where, and Rik wasn't going to yell for him. He didn't want Klik around, even to fetch the crown. Maybe there was a retrieval spell in the magic books!

He hopped up and grabbed one of the dusty tomes, paging through. Hmm . . . spells for turning noses into potatoes, and potatoes into noses. Another spell for putting an itch into someone's shoes—that might be handy to try on Klik if he got too snippy.

Rik sat down at the foot of the throne and pored over the spell.

Ye wizard must first prepare ye elementary charms of Sense, of Shoon, of—

"Shoon?" Rik lowered the book. And what were ele-mentary charms?

He flipped back to the beginning . . . but there, to his

disgust, he found pages of gobbledegook that made "be, bo, booboo, bunk" look easy.

Rik tossed aside the book, got up, and retrieved the crown. This time he'd try not just to hit the emerald he'd picked as a target, but to get the crown to roll back to him.

He did this about a dozen times until he realized that this was even more boring than studying. He needed someone—like Klik—to throw it at! Where was the fun of throwing a crown unless there was a grand chamberlain as target?

He was just reaching for the bell when Klik himself came in, puffing softly and bearing an armload of papers.

Rik threw the crown at him. Klik just tipped his head a little. The crown whizzed past his ear and he kept coming, as if nothing had happened.

"Stand still!" Rik ordered.

"You'll have to use magic to make me, O Great and New Majesty," Klik responded in a reasonable voice. "King Kaliko always permitted me to duck. He said it sharpened his aim."

"Well, fetch the crown back, at least," Rik grumped.

"In a moment, Your Sublime Majesty. Of first importance is this pile of national crises."

"Crises?" Rik exclaimed, sitting up straight. "What? Already?"

Klik shrugged, so that the heavy gold chain round his neck clinked and clanked. "Things move fast in royal circles, Your Percipient Majesty."

Rik eyed his chamberlain. All these additions to his title—rightly his—were maybe just a little too flattering. Was he being made fun of?

"Just 'Your Majesty' will do," Rik ordered as Klik set down the papers on the side table.

"Thank you, Your Majesty," Klik said, and went to retrieve the crown.

Rik took the top sheet of paper off the pile. He frowned. "What is this? I can't make anything out of all this 'theretofore' and 'hitherto.'"

"It is quite clear, Your Far-seeing—ah, that is, Your Majesty."

Rik turned his attention back to the paper "The Kingdom of Ev has trouble with their wheat crop. Too bad. Who cares? What's all this number stuff below it?"

Klik said with a smooth smile, "Well, Your Majesty, due to the failure of crops—very understandable, of course—they fear they must increase the cost of wheat and corn. That means that we are required to supply double the amount of diamonds, triple the number of tourmalines, and quadruple the number of quartzes, in order to get our wheat."

"Wheat? Why do we need wheat?"

"Where do you think our delicious side dishes come from? The tasty crunchiness of fried mushrooms is directly attributable to the corn starch, and as for the wheat, those pies require flour. We cannot grow wheat or corn underground. Not unless Your Majesty wishes to create artificial sunlight, but I fear your subjects would raise great objections to *that*."

Of course they would. Nomes hated sunlight and fresh air, everyone knew that, although Rik had rather gotten used to them during his days of wandering.

Besides, he didn't know the magic to create artificial sunlight. He couldn't even get five basic "b"'s memorized.

"All right, give them their rubies and things," he muttered. "We have plenty."

"It will mean more time in the mines for your people, O Majesty," Klik cautioned.

"Well, what else have they to do?"

Klik sighed, but it was a sigh with a smile just crinkling the corners of his mouth. "Very well," he said. "As Your Majesty commands. Just . . . sign the order, and it shall be carried out."

"I don't have a pen."

Klik whipped one from his pocket.

He held the paper so that Rik could scrawl his name. As Klik blew gently on the paper to dry his ink, Rik scowled at the shaky signature. He would have to practice to make it look big and threatening and kingly, like his father's had.

"All right, what's next?"

"Well, there's a new trade treaty with the Kingdom of Geeki-Goo."

"Geeki-Goo?"

Klik bowed. "We get our fruits from them. For those delicious fruit pies we all love?"

Nomes very much loved baked pastries and tarts and

pies, the sweeter the better. Rik nodded, but then thought of something. He frowned. "Hey, I thought we got our fruit from Ozma. Well, I know we do. She mentioned it was part of the Friendship Pact she made with Kaliko."

"Oh, but Ozma doesn't supply all our fruit. There are so many of us, after all, Your Majesty."

Rik sighed. "So what do they want?"

For answer, Klik held out yet another parchment, which listed fabulous numbers of jewels. Rik sighed as he signed that order. At this rate, he was never going to begin building up his personal treasury.

He heard voices coming from the outer chamber. With a sense of relief, he waved aside the papers.

A moment later his gang came running in. They were all scowling.

"What's wrong?" Rik asked.

"We're not real dukes," Tavi shouted.

"Dukes have to be *of* someplace!" Tavi bellowed.

"They laughed at us!" Wok shrilled. "Said the Nome kingdom doesn't have any dukedoms or earldoms, just rock-domes!"

Where was that Inga when a person needed him? He knew all about dukes and earls and the rest of that court stuff.

Rik turned on the chamberlain. "Where did the girl and boy go?"

Klik looked upward. "I don't know where they might be at the moment," he said. "But I believe they took a tour of Your Majesty's fine kingdom. No doubt they were, ah, shackled by a . . . giant desire to . . . warm themselves at the spectacle of your great inheritance."

Once again Rik had a distinct feeling he was being made fun of. But Klik looked very serious, standing there with his hands folded.

Rik turned his attention back to his impatient courtiers. "Look, you can be Duke of Diamonds," Rik said in a hasty voice. "And you, Tiki, you can be Earl of Emeralds. And you, Tavi—" He paused, unable to think of a title that went with rubies. "We'll come up with good ones for you all. How's that?"

Little Wok piped up. "I want to be grand vizier of gold!"

All the boys turned to Wok. "Grand vizier?"

He put his hands on his hips. "Yes. My ma used to tell me stories from the sunny lands. The Grand Vizier is almost as good as a king, and what's more, he's *always* wicked!"

Jubjub stamped his bare foot. "I don't want to be a duke, I want to be a Grand Vizier!"

"Me too! Me too!" shouted the others.

Rik got up. "It's time for supper," he yelled, and instantly the boys cheered and ran off to the dining room.

Rik followed more slowly, calling over his shoulder at Klik, "See to supper. And make it last!" he added.

"Of course, Your Majesty," Klik responded, chuckling softly under his breath as he smiled down at the signed parchments.

FOR HOURS the poor Tasca
Birds flew an endless series of tunnels, searching for the
pearls.

While Dori and Inga were asleep in the locked chamber,
and Rik and his friends were happily eating their supper,
and Klik scurried to his rooms to plot with his spies, the
birds flew back with empty beaks to the cave where they
had left the Tasca queen.

They cheered at once when they discovered that the
queen had not been idle, despite her long trailing feathers.
She had flown back up the shortest way to the Valley of the
Voe and fetched their favorite seeds and berries, flying back
and forth until she had enough for them all.

With happy trills the birds pecked at the food. Then

they tucked their heads under their wings to get a good sleep before they resumed their search.

A t the same time the birds were settling in for their well-earned rest, Klik was sitting down at his table with his two spies. He had ordered his own minions to set up a fabulous supper. Those stupid boys would never notice the missing food from the royal kitchen. The Nomes toasted each other with three fine goblets of boiled mushroom juice of a royal vintage.

"Now," Klik said jovially as the Lookout and the Long-Eared Hearer rubbed their hands and licked their lips. "Let's eat heartily. We can talk afterward. Here's to a new king, and I do not mean Rikiki!"

He raised his goblet. The other two raised theirs. They all slurped and drank noisily.

"Dig in," Klik said, setting his goblet down. "I'll refill our cups."

He stood up and flourished the jug of mushroom juice. When the Long-Eared Hearer chomped down on some roasted snackleroot, Klik dropped into the spy's goblet a tiny little dried snoozeberry. With his other hand he poured out more juice. Then he moved to the Lookout, and when the spy reached for another helping of pickled wickle grub, again Klik sneakily plopped a snoozeberry into his cup and then poured out more juice.

"I thought I heard wings up thataway," the Long-Eared Hearer said suddenly, pointing behind them and upward. "Probably those stupid Tasca Birds."

And when the Lookout and Klik turned their heads to stare at the ceiling behind them—*Plop! Plop!*—into their goblets the Long-Eared Hearer tossed a dried snoozeberry apiece.

"Now, now," Klik said as he returned to his seat and smiled at his guests. "At least the birds are not bothering us. Remember! No business until we are finished. Let us enjoy our meal, as three friends ought to."

The spies nodded in agreement, and for a short time there was nothing but the sounds of chomping, crunching, and gulping. Then the Lookout said suddenly, "I think I see Kaliko!" He pointed at the entrance to the tunnel.

Klik leaped up, peering, and the Long-Eared Hearer leaned forward, hands over his eyes so he could hear the better. He heard the drip of water, the snoring of some Nome miners four caverns away, and eight caverns and five tunnels downward he detected the distinct sound of Nome girls chasing Hizzard hatchlings, but no Kaliko.

Meanwhile, the Lookout quietly slipped a snoozeberry into each of the others' goblets. "Must have been a shadow," he said, sitting back. "My mistake."

Klik grinned. "Then let us drink to the vigilance of the best spies in the Nome kingdom!" He lifted his goblet to the others.

"Hear hear!"

"See see!"

The three drank all their juice down. Then they picked up their forks.

They chewed.

They swallowed.

Their eyelids fluttered, and *klunk! Klunk! Klunk!*

Three heads thunked onto the table, and there arose the sounds of three snores, the loud snores of peaceful, deep snoozeberry sleep, rattling little stones from the ceiling.

R ik looked around the royal dining room. The boys were mostly done eating, and some of them were beginning to yawn and stretch.

Rik called aside Tiki, who was the most sensible of the boys. "I think Klik has done something nasty to Dori and Inga. As soon as you wake up, take the boys and find them, would you?"

"Who needs them?" Tiki asked with a shrug, stuffing another apple pastry into his mouth.

"I do. I think Klik is trying to bamboozle me. And that Inga does know something about king work."

Tiki nodded. The idea of out-bamboozling Klik instantly appealed to him. "I'll tell the others it's a game of hide-and-find, and that Klik forbids it. That'll get them going for sure."

Rik nodded.

The boys were ready for a good snooze. Since time didn't matter underground, people slept when they wanted to. Rik went off to his new grand bedchamber, and the boys followed, filling up all the guest chambers around the royal bedchamber, which were almost as fine.

After a long game of jumping on the big canopied beds and flinging royal pillows at one another, the boys all settled down, and very soon the sounds of snoring were the only things to be heard in the royal residence.

Rik wandered into the royal wardrobe, where he discovered chests full of costly cloth, most of it gem encrusted and embroidered in gold.

He was going to go right out again, but lingered, scratching his head. He had no interest whatsoever in fancy clothes, but maybe Klik would be a little less snarky if Rik looked more kingly.

He picked out a bright blue silken shirt, a long velvet robe of deep ruby, embroidered with gold and set with diamonds, some voluminous yellow silk trousers, and a pair of emerald-decorated curly topped shoes. Last he found a long green satin sash to tie around his skinny middle, as the tunic had been made to fit a much bigger king.

Laying these out beside the bed for when he woke up to his second day of ruling the Kingdom of the Nomes, he crawled under the covers and dropped immediately to sleep.

Dori woke with a start. "Who's there?" she asked, sleep vanishing.

"Yow! We found 'em! Behind one of the trick passages!"

Boys' voices echoed in cheery triumph.

Dori and Inga scrambled to their feet.

"Come on out," Wok squeaked.

Dori blinked in the bright light beyond, and saw his small figure outlined in an archway.

"Rik sent us to find you," Tiki confided to Dori as the boys surrounded them. "What a fun game! Did ol' Klik do something sneaky?"

"It was he and those two spies," Dori said in a low voice. "You know, the Long-Eared Hearer and the Lookout."

"Oh, them," Tavi scoffed as he skipped backward on Dori's other side. "We call those two the Prime Nosers!"

"There you are," Rik exclaimed as the boys led Inga and Dori into the rich royal caverns. "Just in time for breakfast. Or have you eaten?"

Inga and Dori swallowed, shaking their heads. Dori was amazed. Rik was wearing nice clothes instead of rags, but she didn't say anything. Neither did Inga, though privately he approved. A prince, after all, ought to look like a prince.

Meanwhile, the word "breakfast" had caused a stampede. Rik, Dori, and Inga followed behind the boys through the empty throne room into the dining room, where platter after platter of steaming food awaited.

They all sat down. This time Dori and Inga knew better than to wait politely. It was hard, though, for Inga to grab for his food, as he'd been raised to be courteous. Dori had less of a problem. This is like the lunchroom at school, she thought, and elbowed her way among the boys.

When she had crispy potatoes and several tasty fruit pastries piled on her plate—and Inga's, too—she dug in.

After a time Rik said, "So where did you go? Klik said you were exploring, but he sounded sort of funny. Like he was making a joke."

"Oh, we were exploring, all right," Dori said. "Not that we wanted to. We got put into some trick caverns, all set up to trap people."

"Oh, I know those," Rik exclaimed. "And you got out?"

Both nodded.

"Well, that explains why Tiki wanted to go there first. He has a good sniffer for sneakiness, he does." Rik tapped his nose.

"Well, it's good you've got a Prime Noser on your side, too," Dori said.

The boys agreed with shouts of enthusiasm.

When Rik saw that Dori and Inga were done eating, he said, "You two, come with me. I have some questions."

Inga rose at once, and Dori followed, leaving the boys to start a food fight with the remnants of breakfast. The three retreated to the throne room, where Rik flung himself onto the throne. He tapped the pile of papers still sitting there.

"Do you understand anything about this sort of stuff?" he asked.

Dori took a peek at the topmost paper with its fancy lettering, and shook her head. "Sorry. Trading jewels is not something we study at school."

"Trade is something I know a little about," Inga said modestly. "My father has tutored me in such matters."

"Well, tutor me," Rik said, handing Inga the paper.

Inga read through the entire thing and then set it down. As Rik and Dori watched, he rubbed his chin, then said in a very diplomatic voice, "Did you interview the ambassador of Ev?"

"The who?" Rik asked.

"The ambassador. Ordinarily, protocol requires an interview if a country wishes to alter a treaty."

"Why?" Rik asked.

"Well, a trade treaty is usually brought by an ambassador or a trade deputation." Inga paused. At the others' nods, he went on, "So you can ask questions, and maybe even negotiate—that means make a bargain—before both sides agree to the treaty."

"That makes sense," Rik said. "Sounds pretty boring, though."

"Protocol lessons are not my favorites," Inga replied.

"But they are necessary. You also need to learn geography, and the governmental systems of neighboring kingdoms. I have studied a lot about Ev—have even visited there—and I don't believe I remember any talk of droughts."

Rik sat up straight. "You mean they're lying?"

Inga looked away. In Pingaree no one ever called anyone else a liar. "Perhaps you ought to ask the ambassador from Ev. If there is one."

"You mean, if there isn't one, then someone *here* is making up all this stuff so I sign over a lot of jewels?" Rik asked, smacking the paper. At Inga's shrug, he held out the second paper. "How about this one?"

Again, Inga read in silence.

Then he handed it back to Rik. "I've never heard of Geeki-Goo. Of course I do not know all the kingdoms underground here—"

"But it shouldn't be underground, not if we're getting food from them," Rik said.

Dori crossed her arms. "I think you're right, Rik. Someone's faking these papers in order to pocket all those jewels."

Just then Klik came in with a new stack of papers.

"New papers, heh? How many of these did you fake up in order to get royal jewels for yourself?" Rik demanded.

Klik looked back in vague surprise. He rubbed his eyes, trying to think. He was still very angry. Here he'd gone to all that trouble to put his spies to sleep so he could get all the pearls for himself, and what happened? He slept too!

So he'd sent the two spies to locate Kaliko and see what he was up to. They had to make sure he was well out of the way before they tried to take the throne away from Rikiki. At least Klik was rid of that horrible white pearl and its continuous droning in his ear about how he should restore it and its mates to Prince Inga at once, or there would be terrible trouble. He'd made the Lookout take it, lying about how if the white pearl went far from the others they would lose their power.

Let him listen to that stupid pearl for a while, he thought, and remembered the Long-Eared Hearer. No, let them both listen!

At that thought he was able to smile as he looked at Rik. "How much did I fake up? Oh, most of it," Klik said. "But the ones at the bottom are real."

Dori gasped. "You mean you put lies in all those papers in order to steal Rik's jewels?"

Klik frowned. "Now, now, young lady. First of all, the products of our mines belong to the kingdom. King Rikiki has no personal fortune, as yet. As for me, it's every Nome's right to try to get what he can, if the other fellow isn't smart enough to stop him."

"He's right," Rik muttered. "Just the same, Klik: you're banished."

Klik bowed. "Very well, but who will command the minions to take care of the mess in the dining room, for example? Since you do not know enough magic to make the mess vanish yourself?"

Rik groaned. "Well, then, you're banished to the next room."

Klik bowed and began to retreat.

Rik said, "And take all the papers away that you made to get my, that is, the Nome kingdom's jewels!"

Klik returned, removed three quarters of the stack, and then retreated again. The boys, who had been drifting in one by one (still besplattered with breakfast) began clapping.

"Good one, Rik!"

"That's telling the ol' thunderblunder!"

Rik just ignored them. He turned to Inga. "How do you know all that, about treaties and ambassadors?"

"Well, ever since I was small, my father has given over a portion of every morning to teaching me kingly craft," Inga explained. "In addition to the things I told you about, each day I memorize all the trade tables for the local kingdoms."

"Trade tables!" Rik squeaked.

"Memorize?" Tavi shouted, and he turned a somersault, as thought escaping a terrible monster.

"Then we practice interviewing ambassadors, for they can be very tricky, saying one thing and meaning something else."

"You mean like ol' Klik?"

"Oh, some of them are even worse," Inga said. "My father says that in true diplomatic interviews, you never use one plain word when you can slip in fifty pompous-sounding ones. So we practice. Just the other day it took me fifteen minutes to ask my father how he was feeling."

"Fifteen minutes!" Dori gasped.

Inga sighed. "I am very new to this, which is why I did so poor a job. My father, who is an expert, took a full hour to say 'fine.'"

Rik jammed his elbow on the jewel-encrusted arm of his throne and stuck his chin on his fist. "And then what do you do?"

"We then go over all the internal affairs—in our case, the trade treaties that affect our pearls, which are our chief items of trade. But there are lots of other items of trade business."

"Trade business!"

"Ugh!"

"Boring!"

The boys sent up howls of protest.

Rik ignored them. "And then?" he asked, eyeing Inga.

"And then we have lunch. After which I might practice my fencing, or riding, or else my mother calls me in to practice ballroom dancing—"

"Ballroom dancing! Yuk!" Tavi yelled.

"But you have to know how to dance at the balls that you give to please the nobility and the visiting dignitaries," Inga explained. "Such parties put everyone in a good mood, which makes for more friendly treaty negotiations."

Rik and the boys looked stunned.

Rik said, "I don't think the Nomes have ever had a ball. But I know what they are. Ozma held one, when I was spying on the Emerald City. Music and lots of dancing, and everyone has to dress up in fancy clothes and eat using knives and forks and even spoons."

"Spoons are for better aim when you fling peas," Tiki said. "Useless otherwise."

"Manners?" Jabi groaned. "Horrible!"

"Nasty!" Jubjub clutched his middle as if he had the worst stomachache in history.

"Terrible!" Tavi clawed at his throat, gasping.

"Dreadful!" Wok squeaked, pretending to faint.

Inga said, "Of course, each kingdom is fond of its own customs and considers others' strange. But my father did say to me once that people who are busy dancing in the ballroom all night are too tired in the morning to be out cooking up wars."

"There's something in that," Rik said. "But dancing?"

Tiki snickered. "Imagine my pa wearing velvet like Rik here, and asking Ma to come up from her lair and hop around with him in a big dress! She'd throw him down to the fire pit if he even tried."

Rik got to his feet. "I've made a decision," he announced.

The boys stopped, and on the far side of the throne room, Klik poked his head in.

"So far, being a king has been no fun at all."

"Not for us either," Wok grumped.

"Therefore today I declare a holiday. The Official Day for Having Fun."

Through the sound of the boys' cheering came Klik's

smooth voice. "But Your Majesty, how will the mining get done?"

"It's a holiday for children only," Rik announced. Remembering what Inga had said about keeping people busy, he added, "And the adults can work double to make up."

Inga bent over and whispered into Rik's ear.

Rik frowned at him. "What do you want *them* for?"

"Diplomatic reasons," Inga said.

Rik shrugged. "And Klik, send those two Nosers of yours, the Lookout and the Long-Eared Hearer to me when I get back!"

"As soon as they finish their present work, I promise you will see them," Klik said smoothly.

Inga and Dori exchanged glances. Klik had given in far too easily, and his grin showed way too many teeth for their comfort.

But Rik paid no attention to Dori, Inga, or Klik. With a flick of his wrist, he tossed the crown up to catch on a knob of the high throne and headed out of the throne room. The Nome boys followed with skips, hops, cartwheels, and handsprings.

The other two trailed them more slowly.

"Do you have a plan for getting the pearls back from those two spies?" Dori whispered.

"Not really. All I could think of was to get Rik to order them to be brought to us. But I'm not sure how to get the pearls away from them."

"How about this?" Dori muttered. "I'll ask Rik to get the boys to tackle them hard. Hold them down so we can search them."

"Rik is going to want to know why," Inga warned.

"We can tell him it's a game. Not a great idea, but it's all I can think of. Have you a better idea?"

Inga shook his head. "Not without some time for thought. And it does look like we've got some time now."

"Okay. Think up something better. If you can't, then let's try that."

Inga agreed, but he looked troubled.

When they reached the grand archway leading out of the throne room, Dori glanced back. Klik stood before the throne, laughing.

18

DORI HURRIED to catch up with Rik. She whispered behind her hand, "Klik is up to something."

Rik shrugged. "What can he do? I stopped him stealing the jewels, and I'm king."

Dori shook her head. "I don't know, but I don't like the way he was laughing back there." She pointed back toward the throne room.

Rik grimaced. "Oh, who cares about ol' thunderblunder? Come on, you have to see our oldest game"

"Battle Bones!" the boys all yelled.

And off they ran, down to a huge cavern. As soon as they entered, enormous skeleton warriors appeared out of the walls and began throwing what looked like fireballs at the Nome boys. The boys picked up greenish rocks and hurled them back.

... *enormous skeleton warriors appeared out of*
the walls and began throwing what looked like
fireballs at the Nome boys.

"It's a battle," Rik called, ducking a fireball. "You have to defeat them before they defeat you!"

The fireballs didn't actually hurt anyone. They just made a noise, and the boy hit had to go over to the side until a bell rang.

It was kind of like a live video game, thought Dori. The biggest one she'd ever seen. She looked over at Inga. They both joined in. The boys had not just glowing rocks to throw, but swords of light and coils of glittering rope like snakes.

The skeletons kept popping out, moving faster and faster, but the boys had obviously played for a long time, and slowly they prevailed, until the last skeletons were hit and popped apart, bones clattering, then vanishing back into the walls.

"What now?" Jabi cried.

Dori opened her mouth to speak.

"Let's go," Rik yelled. "I've got a great idea."

"Yay!" the boys cheered. At last, Rik was back to what he did best, thinking up fun things to do!

He led the way down a narrow tunnel to one of the gigantic caverns with a catwalk over it. Down below, Dori and Inga saw countless Nomes busy mining gems, piling the stones in little carts, and sending them zooming by magic along chutes and ramps and tunnels.

Some of the Nomes paused in their work and glanced up at them. None of them was smiling. Dori didn't like the look in those steady eyes, but Rik ignored them all.

"C'mon, don't dawdle," he said, and ran the last of the way across the catwalk, leaving the others to follow.

Dori followed as well, this time glancing up. Something flickered at the corner of her eye, and she canted her head, looking up toward the ceiling far overhead. Two small shapes glided high above—Tasca Birds! Dori had forgotten all about them. She was glad to see that they were all right.

The Tasca Birds were busy with their search. The two that Dori glimpsed looked down, seeing Dori, Inga, Rik, and the boys, and the Nomes. But not the two-legged spies they were searching for.

However, they now had fewer caverns to search. One of them was going to find those spies soon. The thought made them fly the faster.

Rik, Dori, Inga, and the boys emerged from the tunnels on a cliff overlooking a mighty lake below. "Dori," Rik said, "you pick us up and throw us out into the middle."

Dori did not want to explain why she had suddenly lost her super-strength. "I only use my powers when I have to," she said as carelessly as she could.

Rik pursed his lips. "You'll run out of magic if you use too much?"

Dori shrugged.

Rik took that for agreement. "Well then, we'll just dive

off like we usually do. Now! First contest: the funniest dive!"

He jumped off the cliff, wiggling his legs and arms as if he'd been electrified, and fell forty feet or so to land with an enormous splash.

Tavi jumped next, pumping his legs as if trying to run back up into the air. He, too, landed with a big splash.

Dori didn't mind swimming in her summer clothes, which were practically like a bathing suit anyway, but she hated the idea of heavy, squelchy sneakers. So, since there was no blue pearl tucked into her shoe, she sat down and pulled off both socks and shoes.

Inga also took off his socks and shoes, laying them neatly aside. "Thank you for keeping the pearls secret."

Dori nodded. "It's still a good idea. Let's jump in!" She saw Rik watching them, so she marched over and stood at the edge. What made a dive funny? Maybe the boys would think a belly flop funny, but it would sting too much. She could only think of waving arms and legs around.

Whoosh! Through the air, and splash! The water was warm, coming from an underground spring somewhere.

Dori looked up in time to see Inga perform a beautiful dive, except he wiggled his toes, something that wasn't the least bit funny, except maybe to other princes.

Wok came next, crouching into a knot of arms and legs. *Ka-tooosh!* He hit the water hard, sending up a vast spray. At once the game changed, and they all clambered back up, this time trying to make the biggest splash.

As soon as the boys began to tire of swimming, Rik said, "Let's go play hide-and-find!"

He led the way to a cavern near the edge of the lake. Dori and Inga smelled burning rock. A roaring, whooshing sound pummeled their ears, and gusts of hot air blasted out from a great crack in the stone wall. Rik and the boys stood in front of the crack, arms held high. Inga and Dori joined them, and they were all soon dry and warm.

Then they played hide-and-find through the passage-ways, and moved to a cavern that had long abandoned mining equipment on its perimeter. But that was not what drew the Nome boys. They ran past streaks and slides of flat volcanic stone that led to a floor made of smooth volcanic glass. They slid down and down and down, landing in a big pile of feathers, gathered from the mountaintops where the giant gnackle-birds make their nests.

The next game was the most fun of all. The boys ran to where some old bark boards were stacked. They threw these, leaping on them and whooping as the boards slid across the glassy surface of the volcanic lake.

Dori watched for a time. Her attention was caught by the empty chutes and ramps above. On the other side of the cavern a row of little mining carts sat parked and forgotten.

While the boys slid around on the lake, she walked over, bent down, and saw that the wheels on the little carts clipped on. She unclipped four sets of wheels, saw that the clamps were quite sturdy, and carried them to one of the sliding boards. She latched the wheels on, which gripped the long board with a snap of magic.

Snap! Snap! Snap! Snap! Instant skateboard!

Rik, watching from across the room, saw her put the board down, set a foot on it, push with the other, and go whizzing across the lake. He drew in a deep breath. Where had she gotten *that* idea?

Within moments he'd reached the carts, and he, too, soon had a skateboard. The boys watched their king go sliding across the glassy surface at top speed (though his arms windmilled a bit, as he learned to keep his balance) and then gave a huge whoop and promptly joined the fun.

It was Inga who, after studying the surface of the lake, the wheeled boards, and the surroundings, took his board to one of the mine chutes and skated down it. At once everyone had to join him. In no time the boys were inventing tricks, trying to do handstands on their boards, spinning them, hopping up and down.

They played until everyone was so tired they unanimously retreated for a rest on the nest of blankets in the boys' old secret lair.

While they napped, up above, the five Tasca Birds winged their way back to the chamber where the queen awaited them.

"Found them! Found them!" one chirped.

"Spying on king!" shrilled a second.

"Holding pearls," whistled a third.

"Can't get them! Can't get them!" tweeted the fourth.

"Too strong!" warbled the fifth.

The queen listened, then flapped her wings. Her court fell silent. "Plan!" She said, and hopped down to a fine wooden table covered with a silken cloth. "Plan!"

While the Tasca queen chirped her plan to her court, back in the boys' hideout Wok sighed and said, "Time to command ol' Klik to produce some dinner."

"All right." Rik yawned. "We'll have to hike all the way back to the royal chambers."

The boys sent up a groan, and for a time no one spoke.

Then Dori heard a snickery noise. Rik lay there a few feet away, silently shaking with laughter.

Tiki poked him. "What's the joke?"

"I was thinking about king duties. And diplomacy. And dancing."

"Dancing is funny?" Dori asked.

"Yes. At least the idea of ol' Klik dancing around with Jabi's ma."

At once all the boys exploded with howls, yelps, and hoots of laughter.

Wok said to Dori, "She's the fiercest of them all. She's

so fierce, she can make an entire pit of Hizzers faint with just her smile."

"Her smile?" Dori asked.

Tavi shuddered. "My sister is really good at that smile. She once made an entire troop of Dinods stampede, just by twitching her lip."

"Br-r-r-r-r!" Tiki shivered.

But Rik wasn't listening. He jumped to his feet. "Let's go," he said, "before we scare ourselves out of our appetites."

"Now that's a nightmare of a thought," Jabi stated.

They started off on the long walk back to the royal residence. Along the way, as before, Dori glimpsed many Nomes, most peeping from archways and tunnels and sidechambers. Some were still working away with picks and forges and gem-polishing stones, but most watched, their eyes unblinking. None of them smiled or called greetings.

Rik also noticed, and his walk became a swagger of defiance. This was his kingdom. He was not going to be intimidated by lurkings and whisperings and glowers.

They were met by Klik at the huge entrance to the throne room. He was smiling broadly.

Dori hated that smile. "Uh-oh," she murmured to Inga.

Rik's quick ears caught that. "Uh-oh what?"

"I told you I thought Klik was up to something," Dori said.

Rik shrugged one shoulder and pushed past, the boys swaggering right after him.

*. . . Dori glimpsed many Nomes,
most peeping from archways. . . .*

Then he came to a sudden stop, so sudden the boys smacked into one another. There came muffled *Oof!*s and *Ugh!*s, which Rik ignored.

He was too busy staring at the visitors.

There, ranged around the throne, was a waiting group of monsters. Big monsters. Hairy monsters. Scaly monsters. And every one of them grinning.

"Hullo, King Rikiki," growled a giant saurian with at least a hundred teeth, all of them longer than Inga's feet: the King of the Dinods.

"Weee're here to sssssseeee you," hissed a snakelike creature with glowing eyes, a forked tongue, and a lot of arms with grasping, taloned fingers: the Queen of the Hizzers.

But those weren't as scary as the foremost one, a big, hairy two-legged creature with a sneering wolf's head: a Phanfasm.

"We're here," said the Phanfasm, "to declare war on you."

19

BACK IN KANSAS, another winter storm curtained the world with white.

"This weather is awful!" Em's best friend, Claire, exclaimed, running to the window. "I hope I can get home okay."

"We might just have to have a sleepover," Em's second best friend, Anna, said. She grinned. "And I wouldn't mind a bit. I'm sick of being home with nothing to do except argue with my stupid brothers!"

Em looked out at the steadily falling snow. It had cleared enough that morning for her friends to come over for a visit, but that nice blue sky hadn't lasted. Now Em could scarcely see across the street.

She sniffed. "The cookies!" She ran to pull the pan of freshly baked oatmeal cookies from the oven.

"Oh, how I love warm cookies." Anna rubbed her hands.

"Me too." Claire's mouth was full. "Let's take the rest of the batch into the other room and watch a movie."

"Okay," Em said, taking a big bite of a fresh cookie just as the phone rang.

The phone! She stared at it, trying to chew fast.

"Aren't you going to answer it?" Claire asked, calling from the door to the den. "It could be your sister. Maybe she's stuck at her friend's house, like we are here!"

Em muttered, "I wish." Much as she liked Claire and Anna, she knew they would never believe about Oz, so she had told them that Dori was "visiting a friend." Well, it was true, wasn't it?

Trying to swallow her cookie, she picked up the phone. "Hullo." Her voice came out muffled.

"Hey, Dori," Dad said. In the background Em heard a lot of noise, like a crowded train station. "Long time no hear! I was beginning to wonder what was going on there."

I sound like Dori, Em thought, trying to swallow. Tears sprang to her eyes and she almost choked. "I'm fine!" she croaked, trying to lower her voice.

"Got a little cold?"

"Yes." Em hastily shoved the last of her cookie into her mouth. Would that help her sound like her sister?

"Well, I'm not surprised, with this weather. Stay bundled up and warm, hear?"

"Mmm-hmm."

"Now, to business. The planes are still grounded because of the snow, and even the train is stuck, until they can clear the tracks. My cell phone ran out of charge, so I'm stuck here using a booth, and every time I try to call your mom at the hospital, I get a busy signal. So I need you to tell her I will get there as soon as I can."

"Okay, Dad."

"Oop, someone's waiting to use the phone. Kisses to Em," Dad said, and hung up.

Em hung up the phone, her hands shaking. At least that went all right, for once! She glanced toward the other two girls, who were just settling down in the den, Anna going through the collection of movies and reading out each title, and Claire saying either "Maybe" or "Ugh!"

Em ducked into the pantry and pulled the snow globe from her pocket for a quick check. The last two times she'd tried to look into it, nothing had happened. The time before that, she'd gotten the magic to work—just to see Dori asleep in some cave.

Now she wished to see the Emerald City, because the magic worked better there, somehow. She whispered, "Princess Ozma, please let me see the Emerald City."

Lights twinkled and flickered inside the glass, and Em's heart pattered. Good! The magic was working!

But what was that? The towers of the Emerald City shrouded by ugly clouds. Were those the same scary clouds that she and Dori had seen before? There had seemed to be sinister faces in those clouds. She tried to look closer, but the moving vapors shifted and boiled. It almost made her dizzy.

So she looked down below the clouds, to see Glinda and Ozma standing by one of the fountains. Glinda had a wand in one hand, out of which rainbow sparks flew, glittering and gleaming.

They stopped; looked up.

Nothing happened, except the cloud seemed to grow darker, and a strong wind lashed their dresses and hair.

Glinda tossed a powder into the air. It sparked into glittering birds of light. The light-birds sped rapidly in all directions, dwindling to glowing pinpoints of color.

Now the cloud lifted on a wind that caused the trees in the garden to shiver and twist.

Neither Ozma or Glinda moved, gazing steadily upward until the cloud rose high into the sky and the wind slowly died down.

Em groaned, wishing she could hear what they said as they retreated inside the palace. When the last of Ozma's pretty rose gown vanished through the doorway, the cloud overhead had vanished in the distance, and mellow sunlight once again drenched the garden.

Now, that's strange, Em thought—

"What *are* you doing?"

Em looked up, almost dropping the snow globe.

Anna glanced at the snow globe and made a face. "Em, why are you playing with that stupid toy?"

"It's my sister's," she said, knowing that her answer

didn't really make any sense.

But Anna didn't care enough to ask about it. She shrugged, made a disgusted face, then said, "Well, mess with that later, okay? We're waiting for you to vote on these movies we picked. Claire wants one, I want another, and so you have to decide."

Em shoved the snow globe behind a can of corn and shut the pantry door. Before she could join Anna and Claire in the den, the phone rang again.

I'm beginning to hate that phone, Em thought.

She dashed into the kitchen and picked it up. "Hello?"

"Em!" It was Mom. "Does your sister never answer the phone?"

"Anna and Claire are over, and we're right in the middle of making cookies," Em said, again not quite answering the question.

Mom sighed. "Well, don't let your sister spill flour all over, or leave the butter out to turn bad. I would really prefer it if you took charge of the kitchen. Dori is just so forgetful and disorganized." At least she did not add *Just like your father*, Em thought.

"All right, I'll tell them not to make a mess. And I'll take care of the kitchen," she promised, glad to tell the truth for once!

"Now, let me talk to your dad. I have to get our schedules coordinated, and he hasn't bothered to contact me."

Em's relief froze just as hard as one of those icicles hanging from the eaves. "Um—"

"Emma, where is your father?"

More lies flittered through Em's brain like moths caught in a thunderstorm, but none of them landed. Not when she'd been asked a direct question like that.

"He isn't here," she said in a small voice.

"What?" The phone crackled.

"He just called—he said he's tried to call you, but the hospital phone was busy, and his cell phone ran out of charge. He's stuck at the train station—"

"He was supposed to be there today! You *said* he was there!"

"I said he was coming right to us, which was what he thought, too. But then they cancelled the flights, and he was going to take a train instead, and, well, I—*we*—decided it was better not to worry you when Gran was still so sick, since we were all right, and Dad was coming as quick as he could."

"I'm worried *now*." There were crackling noises in the phone, as though her mother were walking back and forth, which she did when she was angry. "Mrs. Gupta says she hasn't been over today."

"She got a cold yesterday, and didn't want to expose anyone," Em said. Her hands felt cold, her mouth dry.

"I think I'd better call her. No, what can she do? Your father has once again managed to leave us high and dry."

Em said unhappily, "It's not his fault; it's the storm's fault!"

Mom sighed, and then said in a tight voice, "It's not

your fault, either. I'm sorry I got snappish. I'm just worried about you girls, is all. I'll be home just as soon as I can. You and your sister can go over to Mrs. Gupta's if you don't like being alone this long."

"Mom, we're just fine, and we don't need to go to Mrs. Gupta's. Nothing has happened except for a lot of snow."

"You shouldn't be alone. I'll be home as quick as I can."

Em hung up.

Trying to pretend nothing was wrong, she walked to the den with the last tray of cookies and sat down on the couch with her guests.

Mom was on her way home! Now what? Well, she was facing the same weather mess that everyone else was. Dori had just better finish up and get back before Mom could actually arrive—before both her parents arrived. Em thought of her father trying desperately to find some way to get here, and groaned.

"Did you eat too many cookies, Em? Got a stomachache?" Anna asked.

"Yeah, right," Em said dismally.

20

THE TWO PRIME NOSERS
had found Kaliko lurking not far from the throne room,
watching what happened inside through a crack and chuckling to himself.

The Long-Eared Hearer and the Lookout, having spotted him, retreated all the way back down to their secret lair
to plan—and promptly began to argue. Because they were
not very smart, their argument tended to go in circles.

"We have to capture him."

"Yes, and you have that strength pearl, so you grab him
and throw him down the fire pit. I'll stay close by with this
pearl, so his magic can't harm us."

(They did not trust each other after the snoozeberry
business, so they refused to carry the pearls in their pockets,

but kept them held tightly in their hands, one with one pearl and the other holding two pearls, and doing his best to ignore the continual warnings of the white pearl that they were about to get into serious trouble.)

"I'm not throwing him in any fire pit. He'll get angry, and even with these here pearls, I don't want him angry at me."

"Fine. So we lock him somewhere else."

"Where?"

"Klik can figure that out. Our job is to capture him!"

"How?"

"Well, say, we throw a blanket over him. You pick him up and hold him with your super strength, and I'll protect us in case he mumbles magic inside the blanket."

"But what if he gets angry?"

"Look!"

"No, you listen!"

"We have to capture him. . . ."

And it would start all over again. The two of them were talking so loud, and glaring at one another so hard, they did not hear or see anything else—not even six birds that came sailing quietly overhead. Four of them flew in a square formation, each carrying a corner of a fancy table cloth in its beak. The center of the tablecloth sagged with its load of little stones that the birds had carefully gathered, but the two Nomes didn't even glance toward the ceiling.

The queen gave a single chirp.

The spies stopped.

"What do you hear?" asked the Lookout.

The Long-Eared Hearer opened his mouth. Too late. They both heard the rattle of many little stones falling just outside the cave. One thing Nomes fear worse than eggs is rockfalls. They whirled around and ran out of the cave—onto the rocky floor covered with small, round pebbles.

Whup! The Lookout, who had gone first, skidded, waved his arms, but he couldn't stop his feet from sliding right out from under him. He yelled, his hand opened, and up flew the pearls he had been holding.

"Here!" the Tasca queen trilled.

And the four birds carrying the tablecloth swooped down, still in formation, and caught the pearls right in the middle of the cloth.

"Yup!" The Long-Eared Hearer was next—his feet scrabbled, sidled, stumbled, and up they flew. As he thumped down onto the stone, he too let go his pearl, and the four birds dove down and caught it in the tablecloth.

"Hey! Wait!" the Lookout yelled.

The birds flapped hard, speeding away.

"Come back here!" the Long-Eared Hearer commanded.

The two got to their feet, started running, slipped on the little round stones, and fell with two thumps. Really angry now, they crawled to the outer tunnel, got up, and started running after those birds.

Up on the higher level where the throne room was located, Dori, Rik, and Inga faced that row of big, grinning monsters.

Rik sauntered right up to the throne and slouched into it, flipping the fringes on his green sash and grinning with challenge.

"If you make war, I'll make it right back," he said. "Klik, blow the whistle. Summon our army."

"But they're all busy in the mines, doing double shifts. On your orders," Klik said with smooth—and very false-sounding—regret.

"Well, summon them anyway."

"That will take time."

"You don't have time," the Phanfasm gloated. "Kaliko forced a treaty on us, but since he's gone, the treaty is too. We love turning Nomes into balls and bouncing them off rocks."

"They are oursssss firssssst," the Hizzer hissed. "Thosssse boyssssss will make a sssssplendid dessssssert."

Rik's friends all scrambled to hide behind the throne. Their heads popped out on either side, looking worried, angry, apprehensive. Tavi muttered, daring anyone to try having him for dessert—though he didn't speak very loudly.

"Do something," Tiki whispered to Rik. "You're the king."

"Like?" Rik muttered back. "Klik isn't taking orders."

"He wants to see you defeated," Inga stated, eyeing Klik.

"Yes," Klik said happily. "It will be fun to watch."

"But we are first," the Dinod growled, stomping forward. Its steps were so heavy that bits of rock clattered down from overhead, and the jewels trembled in their casings. "When we are done working them in our mines, you can have them."

"No, we are first," the Phanfasm declared. "I promised those at home I would use my wicked spells on them to change their forms into something fast, so we can have some sport hunting them before we eat them."

"We are first, or I will pound you into dust," the Dinod declared, standing over the Phanfasm.

"No you won't," the Phanfasm said. His form flickered, and now he was even taller than the Dinod, and his head had changed to a dragon's. His horns brushed the carved ceiling. "Try and stop me now." Smoke trickled from between his yard-long teeth.

"I can stop you both," the Hizzer queen keened, wrapping her long tail rapidly around their legs. "And I will, because *we* are first." At once the two big monsters staggered, almost falling, and both started growling threats at her.

Rik turned to Dori. "Now would be the time to use that super-strength," he muttered.

Dori tried to think of something to say—something to do—but then she heard a familiar flapping sound.

She looked up, and there were the Tasca Birds, arrowing

"Try and stop me now."

down through the apex of one of the great archways, far overhead.

"Dori!" the Tasca queen shrilled. "Pearls! Pearls!"

"What is that bird shrieking?" Rik asked, clapping his hands over his ears.

"Birdsssss good for sssssssssnack," the Hizzer hissed. "Before eat Nomessssssssss." She snapped her jaws and advanced on the throne, slithering from side to side.

Three of the Tasca Birds flew close to Dori. They flapped round and round her, all of them tweeting and trilling sharply, so that it was difficult to see what any one bird was doing. Nomes and monsters all winced from the noise of their screeching.

Dori cupped a hand in front of her, hoping she understood the Tasca queen. Sure enough, one by one the three birds dove down, dropped something from its beak into her cupped hand, and then darted up, shrilling and circling madly about again.

"Thank you!" Dori cried to the birds, who winged toward the ceiling and safety.

Then she turned to Inga, who smiled in relief. Surreptitiously, while the others were still eyeing the birds, she slipped the white pearl to Inga, who was used to talking to it, and shoved the other two deep into her pocket.

Moments later the Long-Eared Hearer and the Lookout arrived, gasping with effort.

The Lookout grabbed Klik. "They outwitted us," he moaned.

"Those nasty birds," the Long-Eared Hearer whined.

"You dolts!" Klik snarled. And in a lower voice, "I told you to give them to me. . . ."

Rik watched, frowning in question. But just as he opened his mouth, Dori said loudly, "You're right, Rik. I think it's time for my super-strength."

She walked forward and bent her head back to gaze up at the glowering Dinod and the towering Phanfasm. "Go away," she said.

They both laughed, exposing teeth as long as her arms. The Phanfasm's fire breath whooshed out, but Dori stood where she was, and the fire did her no harm whatsoever.

The monsters stared in amazement, and the Hizzer queen stopped to watch.

Dori reached forward, put her forefinger on her thumb, and flicked the Dinod's scaly ankle. The creature flew back and landed with such a crash that everyone jumped a foot into the air.

"Your turn," she said to the Phanfasm.

"Oh no it isn't," the Phanfasm declared, arching its gigantic dragon head down, just inches away this time. It gave Dori a mighty blast of fiery breath, with flames that shot out at least twenty feet.

Dori heard Rik and the boys gasp as orange and red and white and even blue flames curled and licked around her. But she just waited, looking at her nails, until the Phanfasm ran out of breath.

"Sssssss!" The Hizzer gave a malicious hiss and darted

her poison-tipped talons at Dori. She smacked them away.

But the Hizzer wasn't done. She was just a few steps from the throne, and turned her head toward Inga, Rik, and the boys, her long tail lashing, her poison-tipped claws reaching—

Dori gave one great leap and landed in the middle of the boys. "Take hands," she whispered.

The boys all had just enough time to grab one another's hands, Dori holding onto Inga on one side and Rik on the other, when the Hizzer whipped her long tail around them all, planning to squeeze them into extinction.

The tail squeezed and squinched until they saw the scales bulging, and the Hizzer queen grunted and fumed with effort.

Nothing happened.

When the Phanfasm saw that the Hizzer was having no luck, it roared with laughter and once again tried its dragon breath, this time trying to fry the entire group.

"Ghack!" Wok yelled. "What have you been eating? Stinkberries?"

"Get your tail off of us," Dori said to the Hizzer queen, "or I'll tie it into a bowknot."

BLAM! The Dinod ripped a gigantic stone from the wall and threw it with all its colossal strength right at Dori and the group.

The boys ducked, but Dori raised a fist and punched the flying rock, and the stone smashed into a million bits of sand, which landed harmlessly in piles all around the edges of the throne room.

Dori was just beginning to enjoy herself when she realized the Phanfasm and the Dinod were still grinning. Moments later the archways all darkened, and there stood about a hundred Dinods, all of them waving sharp weapons.

Then they surged and shifted, and Phanfasms appeared among them, also carrying weapons, their animal heads grinning.

And in the back came the hissing of a hundred Hizzers.

"Yes." The Phanfasm chief laughed. It was a very nasty laugh. He rippled back into his favorite form, a huge, hairy fellow with a wolf's head. "You can fight against us one at a time, but you can't defeat us all."

"What do you want?" Rik asked, taking a defiant stance in front of Dori and Inga.

"Just a new treaty," the Phanfasm said with a cruel, howling laugh. "We want lots of your Nomes in order to wait on us hand and foot, so we can devote all our time to wickedness. Much more fun."

"We want Nomes for snacks," the Dinod growled. "We're sick of vegetables."

"We want Nomesss to sssship to the Sssssspider-Batsssss," the Hizzer jeered. "You do not want to know what the Sssssspider-Batsssss will do to them . . . and we do not care, sssso long as they don't do it to ussss."

"But that's not a treaty," Rik said, looking pale. "We don't get anything out of it."

"Oh yes you do," the Phanfasm declared. "We shall leave the rest of you alone, and only take half of your caves and jewel mines."

"But that's not fair," Inga protested.

All the monsters laughed.

The Dinod finally growled, "What a delightful word. 'Fair.' I'll have to remember it when next we need a good joke."

And the Phanfasm said, "There's no such thing as fair. Only strong, and stronger."

"Yes," said a new voice. "And I'm the strongest of all."

Everyone turned around, staring in surprise. There, at the very back of the room, having stepped through a modest door in one of the stone walls, was—

Kaliko!

21

KLIK SAID you were no longer king," the Dinod snarled.

"True," Kaliko said. "But I still have magic."

"What can you do against all of us?" the Phanfasm roared, waving his powerful arms.

At once a hundred Phanfasms crowded right into the room, and more appeared behind them in every tunnel and doorway all around the throne room, brandishing swords, knives, and spears.

"And us?" the Dinod shouted, clapping its terrible claws with a loud clacking noise.

Through the multitude of Phanfasms thrust a hundred huge, muscular Dinods, each equipped with sharpened teeth and claws.

"And usssss?" the Hizzer sizzled, slapping her tail on the stone floor.

With a sliding, swishing noise, Hizzers now appeared everywhere, tails lashing, poison-tipped claws held at the ready on each of their many arms, as they squeezed between the other monsters.

"What can I do?" Kaliko asked, standing right next to the throne. "This."

He snapped his fingers.

Thunder roared, the air filled with greenish light, and smoke blasted down from the ceiling, smelling to Dori of the school lunchroom on "cabbage and casserole surprise" day, and to Inga of old towels left unwashed and forgotten in the bottom of the rowboat. Even Rik held his nose.

As the thunder died away to a low rumble, the throne room was filled with the sounds of loud sneezes from Dinods, hissy coughs from the Hizzers, and rasping, choking noises from the Phanfasms.

"While they are busy," Kaliko said to Rik, "perhaps we might do a little negotiating of our own."

Rik looked around. "Negotiating? I think I've been cheated enough."

"Not by me," Kaliko said, looking surprised.

"By him," Rik said, pointing at Klik, who gazed up at the ceiling.

Kaliko smiled.

"And them," Dori added, pointing at the Prime Nosers and thinking of the pearls.

Now Kaliko pursed his lips, facing the last two. "Really?"

Whatever deals had been made between Klik and his former king obviously hadn't included the Prime Nosers. They looked around guiltily.

"Whatever happens," Kaliko said, "perhaps our enterprising counselors here will better remember their jobs if they begin by having to scrub the royal dining room—by hand—for the next six centuries."

"Nooo! Not that!" the Lookout gasped.

"Anything but that!" the Long-Eared Hearer moaned. "We've worked hard for you, and what's wrong with trying to get some magical power for ourselves? It's hallowed Nome custom!"

"Not if you get caught," Kaliko said. Then he relented and said, "Six days, then. Anyway, Rik, it comes down to this: I have magic. You don't. You won't get rid of those fellows except by having more power than they do." He pointed at the assembled enemies, who still stomped around, trying to mop streaming eyes and wave away the smelly smoke.

"What do you want?" Rik asked.

"My kingdom, and you drop your claims."

"And if I don't agree?"

"Then I step aside and let you deal with the monsters."

"You won't help me?"

"No."

Dori flushed with affront on Rik's behalf, and Inga

looked sad, but Rik's band weren't the least bit surprised. It was Nome custom.

"Give me a moment," Rik said finally.

"All right," Kaliko said. He snapped his fingers again—and this time there was a blast of orange smoke, and the air reeked of fake perfume to Dori, and of rancid candies to Inga.

Howls of protest and disgust arose from the visitors, and once again they stomped, coughed, sneezed, and groaned.

Rik waved to his friends. They all huddled around the throne. "All right," he said. "You're all counselors. Counsel."

"Fight 'em," Jubjub snarled, waving a fist.

"With what? Klik still has the whistle."

"I could go get my sister," Tiki offered. "You know the girls always like a good battle."

Rik nodded. "Even Phanfasms are scared of our females."

"But what if they decide they like it up here in the mines, instead of away in their own secret lair? What if they decide to take over the mines as well as the jewel making? No one would ever defeat *them*," Jabi said.

Rik said, "Hmm. This is true."

The boys were silent.

Inga tipped his head. "If you wish the advice of an old, wise, honorable magical object—"

Rik shook his head. "No. I don't want the advice of

magical objects, especially honorable ones. I want real advice." His slanty gaze turned Dori's way.

Dori realized that this was what Ozma had foreseen all along, that Rik might in some way get his throne back—but he wouldn't be strong enough or mean enough to hold it against all the enemies of the Nomes. If any of them took over the Nome Kingdom, they would probably force all those Nome miners up to the surface to do their conquering for them while they gathered up all the gems and jewels.

Dori motioned to Rik, and he leaped off the throne. The two of them moved a little ways away, as the sounds of whooping and sneezing faded behind them.

"Listen, Rik, you really hate all the boring parts of ruling, right?"

He shrugged—but did not disagree. "So?"

"So you don't really know what you're doing, either. Why not just give up the throne?"

"But I hate letting Kaliko get the best of me." Rik shrugged. "I think I can beat those creeps. Not with magic, but if I get the females up—some of my girl cousins could wipe up those Dinods in an eyeblink—and then maybe I could try some other tricks—"

"Maybe you can," Dori said. "But after? What about all the treaties, and the trade, and the magic words, and the rest of it? Are you ready to do that every day, from now on?"

Rik waved a hand. "That was just Klik's trickery."

"The Ev treaty was fake, and that other one about the fruit, but all the rest were real enough. Like Inga told you, and you know *he* doesn't lie, being a ruler is hard work, which has to be done every day. That means always being prepared."

Rik grimaced.

Dori added, "And being prepared means you have to work to *get* prepared."

Rik sighed. "I hate work."

Dori said, "Look. You Nomes live a long time. Kaliko wants to be king again, and he seems to do a good enough job. At least, nobody was complaining when we came. So what would be wrong with going back to your adventures? He might get sick of it someday and ask you to come back."

Rik put his head to one side.

"Maybe by then you'll be ready for boring magical studies, and diplomatic talk, and treaties, and all the rest."

"Rikiki?" Kaliko called. "I won't wait much longer, and neither will these fine fellows, unless I miss my guess."

"All right," Rik said in a short voice.

In silence he held out the crown to Kaliko, who took it with a smile and a slight, mocking bow.

Kaliko clapped the crown onto his head and sat down on the throne.

Dori watched closely. This time, when he snapped his fingers, she saw him press the other hand against one of the jewels under the arm of the throne.

Again the air filled with smoke, this time purple, and a nasty smell of moldy pumpkins added its presence.

"You violate the rules of warfare," the Dinod chief howled in protest. "Forbidden by treaty is the torture of the thousand stinks!"

"Who was that laughing about the word 'fair' a while ago?" Kaliko responded with his customary cheer. "Let's see, I think it's about time for smell number nine-hundred-ninety-six: sour and unwashed stenchbug nest—"

"No! Anything but that!" the Phanfasm shouted. "Attack!"

Kaliko shifted his hand under the throne arm, raised the other hand, and snapped three times. To everyone's amazement, the spears and truncheons brandished by all the armed minions turned into bubbles.

Whish, pop! Whish, pop! The Tasca Birds darted about, bursting every bubble that wobbled near them.

The Hizzer queen clacked her poison talons and pointed at the group near the throne. "Attack!"

Four finger snaps this time, and lights flashed around all the Hizzers. When everyone else had blinked away the brightness, they saw tiny lizards on the ground where the Hizzers had once stood.

The Hizzer-lizards scampered away, vanishing down the tunnels.

"Now, let's see. . . ." Kaliko mused. "The Dinods would make fine goldfish for my pond, and as for the Phanfasms, what could be more useful than a bushel of potatoes?"

Gasps from the enemy.

"All right," the Phanfasm chief groaned. "You win."

"Yes, I rather think I do. We'll revert to our old treaty, then?"

"Yes."

"So that means you are trespassing on our land, uninvited, and that breaks the treaty, which gives me the right to—"

"We're gone!" the Phanfasm yelled, and the next sound was that of stampeding Phanfasm feet.

"As for the Dinods—"

Their chief didn't even stay long enough to reply. The throne room shook and trembled, tiny rocks sifting from above, from the thumping of thousands of big scaly feet trundling away as fast as they could go.

When the trembling of their retreat died away, Kaliko snapped his fingers again, and the drifting smoke vanished.

K ALIKO SETTLED the
crown more firmly on his head and rubbed his hands.

"Now, who is hungry?" he asked. "I don't know about
all of you, but all that magic makes me ravenous. Shall we
have a banquet?" He turned to Rik's band of friends.
"You're all invited."

They sent up a cheer, and Kaliko snapped his fingers at
Klik, who scurried out to see to it. By the time they strolled
into the dining room—where the Lookout and the Long-
Eared Hearer stood by with mops and pails—the great
gem-studded platters were already being borne in.

"I think he tricked me from the start," Rik muttered to
Dori, making an angry face.

"I do too," she replied. "But do you really want to stay
here and do all those kingly things?"

"I could get used to it."

"And you still could, someday. Why not have fun until then?"

Rik looked a little less sour. "Only real problem is the boys. They'll be disappointed."

"Are you sure? I didn't think they liked you being king. I mean, the things they liked best—playing the games—you do anyway."

Rik cocked his head. "Think so?"

"Ask them," Dori said as they all sat down.

The food was delicious, and perhaps because Kaliko was there—and he'd done all that magic—even the boys used a semblance of manners, so this time Inga and Dori got plenty to eat. The Tasca Birds darted down and got grapes and other tidbits to bring to the Tasca queen, who perched on a chair against the far wall.

"So," Kaliko said after the last of the desserts had been carried away. He got up and led the way to the throne room. Behind them the sounds of sweeping and scrubbing began. "What will you do next?"

Rik gave him a challenging smile. "I take it you don't want me around, is that it?"

Kaliko shrugged. "You never did your studies, and you were always playing hooky from mine duty. Are you just going to run around in the caves playing hide-and-find with the Hizzers? They will get their shape back when the spell wears off, I might add, and their tempers will not be so good."

The boys all turned to Rik with expectant faces.

Rik glanced Dori's way, then said, "You know, I really liked exploring on the surface. I think I'll go back up and find some more adventures." He said to the boys, "How does that sound?"

Tiki grinned. "You mean we can come with you?"

"Sure. Why not?"

Jubjub promptly did three handsprings and a cartwheel. "Yippee!"

"It's so boring here without you," Wok piped up. "I want adventures!"

"Me too! Me too!" shouted the others.

"Well, then, why not get started?" Kaliko invited. "On the surface it is still day, and this girl can get you all past the Iron Giant." He pointed at Dori.

Rik nodded. "Nothing worth waiting for. Get anything you want to take," he said to the boys. "I'm going to get rid of this king gear. I want my regular duds!" And he ran off himself.

The others scampered off in several directions, leaving Dori and Inga with Kaliko.

Dori watched the Nome king pull a pipe from one pocket and a live, burning coal from another. He lit the pipe and sent smoke curling up toward the ceiling, then turned to Dori. "Well? I sense you have something to say."

Dori had been thinking hard. She had a pretty good idea of "Nome custom" by now, which meant they could cheerfully lie and cheat one another. Unless, of course, someone had the upper hand.

She said, "I think you set up all those spells beforehand. I think it probably took days of work, too. I don't believe you can do all those mighty spells with finger snaps. And I saw you doing something there, under the arm of the throne."

Kaliko sent another smoke ring snaking up through the air. "And what if that's true?"

"You could have told Rik about those spells and let him use them."

Kaliko shook with silent chuckles. "No. I did the work, so I had the fun. One of the rules of kingship that Prince Inga didn't mention."

"So you were spying on us all along?"

"Of course. I knew Rikiki wouldn't last long."

"I figured your giving up easily was some kind of trick."

"Enough of that," Kaliko said, waving his hot coal. The smell of burning rock tickled Dori's nose. "I've also had enough truth for one day. I will ask you one last question, and I will answer one last question from you. Agreed?"

Dori nodded.

Kaliko dropped the hot coal into his pocket. "So what are you really here for?"

"Princess Ozma sent Inga and me here to help Rik gain his kingdom if he could, but what she mostly wanted to avoid was a Nome war with your neighbors."

"Ah." Kaliko nodded. "And *your* question?"

"I want to know if you've seen Princess Dorothy. She's

supposed to be somewhere surrounded by gray, Ozma said. I wondered if it might be here in your kingdom."

"No," Kaliko said, shaking his head very fast. "I don't have her here. Further, I wouldn't want her around. That little girl is very unlucky for Nomes."

On Kaliko's other side, Inga nodded. The white pearl had just told him Kaliko was speaking truly.

Dori understood the nod, and sighed a little.

Kaliko smiled. His eyes were crinkled with good humor, but his gaze was quite shrewd. "You can also tell Ozma that I do appreciate her noninterference, and I will remember it. Which, for now, means we'll go back to living as we have, and the neighboring lands—I mean the quiet ones on the surface, like Pingaree—won't hear anything from us, except on regular trade days."

Dori nodded, saying out loud, "I'll tell her." She was glad that this part of her quest had ended satisfactorily, but she'd hoped to be able to bring a smile to Princess Ozma's face by carrying back news of Dorothy.

The boys returned just then, some of them carrying little bags or pouches, most of them carrying their new skateboards. Rik once again had on an old long shirt and some trousers slightly less raggedy than his former ones.

Kaliko said with great cordiality, "I shall escort you to our borders myself."

"Want to make sure we're gone, eh?" Rik asked, grinning.

Kaliko bowed, a very ironic bow, but he grinned back.

They soon reached the tunnel that led to the mountainside. In fact, they reached it so soon that Dori suspected magic here, too. But the boys didn't say anything. They were too busy talking about what they'd like to see first, and do first.

A familiar thumping smote their ears as they emerged into a warm afternoon with fragrant soft breezes and slanting golden light. Kaliko waved, and behind him Klik waved too, and then they started down the trail.

Dori stopped the hammer, as before, and all the boys filed past. She let it go, then jumped when it landed behind her with a loud *WHUMP!*

She couldn't help a glance back up at the mouth of the cave, where Kaliko stood, rubbing his chin thoughtfully. Then he waved the stem of his pipe, turned, and vanished.

"Where first?" Tiki asked, rubbing his hands.

"Oh, let's go north," Rik said, waving. "I've never tried that direction."

At once Rik's band of friends turned northward, some of them hopping, some jumping, and Jubjub turning an occasional handspring.

"Hey, there's a flat path down," Jabi called. "We can skate!"

Rik lingered, facing Dori and Inga.

"So I didn't keep my throne," he said. "But you were

TROUBLE UNDER OZ

pretty good, there, at the end."

"That last part was kind of fun," Dori said.

Inga looked from one to the other, and realized that Rik seemed to want to say something, but he wasn't going to say it with Inga around. "I'll look for our magic carpet," he suggested, kind and polite as always.

As soon as he had gone around a big boulder, Rik sighed. "He was a help too, but he makes me want to bite everyone who smiles and kick everyone who is kind."

Dori couldn't help but giggle. "Well, he's been raised as a proper prince. That's what they're like, I suspect. Kind of wearing on the rest of us. I mean, he'd never drop his salad on his lap or sneeze during a long speech. And I'll bet he really does know all the trade tables by heart."

Rik shrugged. "If you're hinting around about what kind of king I should be someday—"

"Nomes are different," Dori said quickly. "No hints."

Rik looked over his shoulder at the trail to the north, then back, and said quickly, "If you ever need help, find me. If I can help, I will."

Dori could see that he was serious, but she knew him well enough by now to know that he hated being serious— or being caught at it. So all she said was "I'll remember."

Without another word he ran off, yelling, "Tiki! Tavi! Wait up!"

Dori walked around the cliff side and soon found Inga, who had the carpet spread out, and Jellia Jamb's empty basket sitting on it.

Overhead, there was a whirring noise.

The Tasca Birds had followed them out through the tunnels into the air, and had been flying quietly overhead. Now the Tasca queen fluttered down, landing for the last time on Dori's arm.

Dori was glad of that blue pearl when the heavy bird landed. She also knew her duty. Rik might hate things like "please" and "thank you," but the Tasca queen wouldn't.

"You saved me," Dori said to the Tasca Bird. "*And* the pearls. I thank you."

"You saved our greatest treasure," Inga said, bowing low and flourishing his cap. "Thank you."

"Fun!" the Tasca queen shrilled, and above her, the court cried, "Fun! Fun!" She then looked at Dori from either side of her head. "Honor! Promise!"

"Yes, you did keep your promise, in the most honorable way," Dori said. "Thanks again, and farewell!" She tossed the Tasca Bird up for the last time and watched the beautiful rainbow feathers streaming out until the birds were out of sight around a snowy peak.

"Off to Pingaree!" Dori said, climbing onto the magic carpet next to Inga.

The carpet lifted up and began to sail gently over the mountains toward the bright blue Nonestic Ocean. Once they were in the air, Dori handed over the pink and blue pearls to Inga, who took them and placed them in the velvet bag, and stored the bag safely in his tunic.

The sun had set behind them when they drifted down to the royal palace of Pingaree. The arched windows were lit with golden light, the silhouettes of people moving behind them. Faint strains of music, tootling flutes and rippling violins, rose on the soft night air, and Dori and Inga knew that this season's crop of duchesses and dukes were happily dancing away at a grand ball.

Beyond the palace, the forest rustled peacefully in the cool sea breeze. Faint stars twinkled above the trees. And below, glimpsed through the tree branches, were glimmers of light from the homes of the ordinary folk who would be dukes and duchesses next season.

Good smells wafted out onto the terrace as Inga and Dori climbed off the carpet. Once again, a tall steward appeared.

"You are back, Prince Inga and Miss Dori," he said in grave tones.

"We are indeed, Gimplik," Prince Inga replied with equal gravity. "Will you report to my royal parents that we are safely returned?"

Gimplik the steward bowed. "I have instructions from Queen Garee that upon your return you are to be offered refreshment, during which time I shall apprise the king and queen of your return."

"Thank you," Inga replied, again gravely, and Dori

chimed in with a cheery "Thanks!"

The steward left, and Inga whispered behind his hand, "At least we get to eat before the questions start."

Dori snickered, and the two went inside the royal residence part of the palace. The musical tinkle of crystal and the laughter of guests were louder as they ran up the marble steps to the bedchambers.

Dori went to her room, looked around for a bath, saw a pitcher with a pretty sign that said "Cleaning Wings," and poured it out.

At once millions of glowing butterflies streamed out, brushing their soft wings all over Dori and her clothes, leaving her fresh and clean.

She met Inga outside in the marble hallway.

Together they ran down again, to find the king and queen both awaiting them in what Inga called the "small dining room," though it was as big as Dori's entire house back in Kansas.

Once again the gold plates appeared with delicious foods on them, and Dori and Inga took turns eating and talking.

"So I never actually met any girls, except for one who was invisible," Dori said to the queen as she finished up her part of the story. "But I never met any Nome girls at all. And from the description, I'm not sure I would want to!"

"They sound quite fierce," Queen Garee replied. "Yet from what you two have gathered, it is they who practice the arts of cutting the gems that the men mine."

Dori nodded. "And from what the boys said, it was the Nome girls who invented the little cart game at the volcanic lake." She grinned, thinking that it was yet another girl—Dori herself—who had showed them how to make skateboards.

On the other side of the table, Inga was saying, " . . . so I told Prince Rikiki that he must learn to negotiate. But that was before I saw the style of negotiation usually practiced between the Nomes and the Dinods and the rest."

After Inga told his father about what happened in the throne room, King Kitticut laughed. "Negotiation indeed! No wonder they were astonished at your suggestion of using social engagements to help with diplomacy."

Inga nodded. "I confess I cannot envision King Kaliko asking the Hizzer queen to dance."

King Kitticut laughed louder, and Queen Garee shook with mirth. "No, no," she said. "Nor the Phanfasms properly utilizing their silverware at table, or the Dinods learning the art of the courtly bow."

They all laughed at the idea, and chattered a little more. Inga and Dori were tired after their long adventure, and so they decided to go to bed, while Inga's parents returned to their party.

Dori yawned as she climbed the stairs to her guest room. She jumped into the big bed and snuggled down.

Her last thought was: Tomorrow Ozma—and then home.

23

Em stood at the window and stared in dismay at the taxicab just arriving. Mom was home!

Em stared for a couple of seconds as her mother paid the driver and then got out her suitcase. What now?

Em ran upstairs. She stopped by the linen closet for towels and then ran into Dori's room, flung back the covers on the bed, and put the towels down, plumping them hastily into more or less a kid shape. Then she stretched the covers up over the pillow, looked doubtfully at it, and pulled Dori's curtains closed.

There. In the dark it looked sort of like a kid asleep—if that's what you expected to see.

Em shut the door, her heart racing, and ran downstairs again, this time hustling through the kitchen. She put two bowls in the sink and ran water on them, along with two spoons, and set the table for two.

She'd just finished when she heard the front door open, so she ran into the living room. "Mom!" she cried.

"I'm home, girls," Mom said, pausing to kiss Em's forehead and then dumping her suitcase down. "At last I had one piece of luck. A very nice man at the hospital, who I saw every day visiting his father with a broken leg, turned out to be a pilot for a private airline. He offered me a ride home as soon as the airports were cleared, since there were no flights to be had into next week. Did your dad arrive?"

"No. He might still be stuck in the train station."

Mom looked mad, then just tired. "I really need some coffee," she said, walking into the kitchen. "Well, it doesn't look bad at all. You did a good job, girls. Dori?" She looked around. "Where's Dori?"

"Upstairs," Em said.

"She doesn't want to come down and say hello?" Mom frowned a little.

"She might still be asleep."

"But there are breakfast things here," Mom said.

"I know—I was just about to wash them," Em said.

"At noon? Goodness, you girls did get lazy. Not that I blame you, considering what the weather has been like. But Dori really doesn't need to sleep all day," Mom said, starting up the stairs.

"Oh, but she does," Em said, lowering her voice to a whisper, as if Dori could hear.

Mom opened Dori's door, peered in, and frowned. "Good grief, it looks just like it did when I left. She wasn't exactly a help in the cleaning, I take it."

"Oh, she was fine. Downstairs. Just not here," Em whispered.

Mom said, "Dori!"

Em groaned. "Don't wake her up!"

"Why not?" Mom turned around, looking suspicious, but at least she shut the door.

"Dori stayed up all night. She did an adventure movie marathon, and then she ate breakfast and went to bed."

Mom laughed—and turned away. "Now that sounds just like Dori! Well, I can't be mad. It is vacation, and you girls haven't gotten to do a single fun thing that we'd planned."

Em sagged against the wall in relief.

"Let me get my clothes into the washer and fix some coffee, and maybe Dori will be up by then," Mom said.

"Don't you want to take a nap?" Em asked.

"I did, on the endless taxi ride from the airport," Mom said. "You should have seen what a mess the roads were! Once that's done, I'll need to call your Aunt Susan and give her the latest report on Gran. . . ."

Mom kept chattering about traffic, snow, and travel while she got her suitcase and took it down to the laundry room.

Em, trembling with relief at the close call, but worried about what would happen next, ran back to the kitchen to get the snow globe.

She locked herself into the bathroom and crouched over it.

"Princess Ozma, please let me see Dori?" she whispered. "Oh, Dori, I need you home *now*!"

R IGHT AROUND that time (if you can measure time that runs sideways), Dori was crossing the Deadly Desert on the magic carpet.

She'd seen the mermaids splash when the sun came up, had a royal breakfast with Inga and his parents, then said her good-byes. The last thing she heard as the flying carpet rose up from the terrace and wound around the golden domes were the voices of Inga and both his parents wishing her a fair journey and inviting her to return.

"I'm almost home," she said to the carpet. "I wonder how Em is doing?"

It was great to be in Oz, she'd decided, but not without her sister. As the wind whistled past her, ruffling her braids, she clutched Jellia Jamb's basket—full of good things to eat on the long journey—and thought about the adventures.

She'd done many things—helping the freshwater mer-folk, and the Tasca queen, and Rik. But somehow things didn't feel right. They didn't feel *finished*.

She frowned. "I think it's that I expected somehow to be the one to find Dorothy."

But maybe someone else had, so why did she feel that things weren't right? She looked around fearfully for one of those terrible clouds that moved so fast. None in sight.

And none appeared during her journey back to the Emerald City, to her relief. She ate her lunch as she crossed over the pretty valleys, rivers, and forests of Oz, all bright with flowers and odd-looking little villages here and there. Once she saw a castle that seemed to be made of patch-work, reminding her of Scraps the jolly Patchwork Girl.

At last she spotted the lovely green towers of the Emerald City on the western horizon, and the carpet started its slow descent.

The first person she saw was Scraps, dancing out to greet her, bright button eyes gleaming merrily in the sun-light.

"Hullo!" she cried.

"Hi, Scraps," Dori exclaimed, climbing off the carpet, which rose and sailed away to its storage place. "Did any-one find Dorothy?"

"No," Scraps cried, quite cheerfully. "I'm sure she's having fun somewhere."

"You're not worried that she's lost?" Dori asked as she followed Scraps inside the palace.

*Once she saw a castle that seemed
to be made of patchwork. . . .*

Scraps skipped along, her colorful patched skirts swinging like a bell. "Not a bit," she exclaimed. "See, I figure it this way. She knows where she is, so she's not really lost. Button Bright taught me that, you see. But we don't know where she is, so we're kind of the ones lost, but since we're home, in our favorite place, we don't feel lost. So everyone is fine."

Dori tried hard to unscramble that, and finally laughed, shaking her head.

She was still laughing when Ozma came out of her dining room to greet her. "Dori. Welcome back. How was your journey?"

The two walked out into the rose garden as Dori told Ozma all about her adventures. Ozma listened in thoughtful silence, paying close attention as she always did.

At the end, Dori said, "So I don't really feel the adventure is finished, somehow."

Ozma smiled, bending to untangle a dangling vine filled with lavender blossoms from one of the peach-colored roses. "Perhaps your adventure isn't finished," she said. "Though I think this portion of it is. Inga, after all, would say it's done, would he not?"

"Yes," Dori said, thinking back. Inga had come along to give advice in a matter of kingship, the matter had been decided, and so he was done.

Ozma nodded. "Just think. Someone's adventure is beginning today. Someone else's is finishing. Dorothy seems to be in the middle of one, and so are you. Maybe it's the same one. Adventure," she added, "is very grand: it never quite ends, really. It just braids itself between different people. We only think it ends, when our part is done and we settle down cozily in our rooms and look back."

Dori thought it over. "So you think we will be able to come back to Oz, then?" She amended conscientiously, "Or, at least, Em could, since I just had my turn?"

For answer, Ozma lifted from around her own neck a medallion. It was heavy gold, with tiny emeralds set all around the center. "I saw you coming in my Magic Picture," Ozma explained as she handed Dori the medallion. "Glinda just finished making this for you. It will enable you both to return to us in Oz, as long as you are together, whenever you see the need. Glinda says that she is in the middle of a very . . . challenging adventure, and in the future might not be able to set up the magic to bring you over as she did this time."

Ozma was trying not to worry her. But it didn't work. "It's Dorothy, isn't it? Something's wrong."

Ozma put her head to one side. "No, and yes. The yes part is that she can't seem to get home, and the no part is that I've heard her voice, through magical means. Once just last night. Her adventure is a long one!" She leaned forward and kissed Dori on the forehead. "You have done well, and we will see you again, I am sure. But now it is time for you to return home." She leaned forward and whispered the magical spell for using the medallion.

Dori said the spell back, meaning to practice—and to

her surprise, the world began to swirl around her full of bright colors.

Knock knock!

Em opened the front door a crack.

"Dad!"

"Didn't expect me, huh?"

"I thought it would be Mrs. Gupta," Em exclaimed, throwing the door open and leaning into her father's open arms for a hug.

Dad chuckled as he let her go, and Em, though she was glad to see him, sneaked a troubled look at his smiling face. Now she had both parents home, which meant she had the problem of two parents asking questions she couldn't answer.

Dad finished stomping his feet on the mat outside the door, then stepped in. Em sprang to close the door. "Someone needs to shovel that walkway, and I guess that someone will have to be me. But first, to kiss my girls. I'm sorry it took so long to get here."

"Oh, we were all right," Em said. "Mom got here this morning."

Mom appeared in the hallway right then. "So you made it after all," she said.

"Train, bus, car, everything but bicycle and horse," Dad

said. "I'm sorry I was late."

"Well, it seems the girls were fine on their own. But Dori is still asleep," Mom said, frowning. "She's slept all day. I ought to go upstairs and find out if she's sick."

"I'll go," Em exclaimed. "You fix Dad some coffee or something."

"I wouldn't mind," Dad said, carefully polite.

Em didn't wait to hear Mom's answer—she just ran.

"Now what?" she said aloud when she got to Dori's room. "Now what?"

She flung the covers off the bed, put the pillows back where they belonged, and then ran into the bathroom. This was the last brilliant idea she could come up with. "Dori, you better come home," she muttered, running the bathwater.

And when the sound of footsteps thumped on the stairway, Em called down, "She just went to take a bath! She said she'll be right down!"

Dad laughed. "All right." He started back downstairs.

Mom said a lot less cheerfully, "She might have bothered to say hello first."

Em leaned against the door, groaning. What else? Dori couldn't take a six-hour bath. They were in trouble. She could see all too clearly Mom's angry face getting angrier and angrier if she tried telling the truth. It was too easy to imagine the police being called, the neighbor yelled at, being grounded for the rest of her life—

Em felt tears burning her eyes, blurring them so much she almost missed the flash of green light in Dori's room.

But she rubbed away the prickle of tears and realized that she *had* seen that flash.

She lunged into Dori's room in two giant steps, and there was her sister, blinking as she looked around.

Em eased the door shut, then exclaimed, "Oh, finally!"

Dori grabbed her in a crushing hug, and Em squeezed her sister back until they both had to let go and catch their breath.

Em just stood there, not sure whether to laugh or cry or both. Her knees felt kind of watery and her throat ached.

Dori rubbed her eyes, then said with concern, "Uh-oh, are we in trouble?"

Em gulped in a deep breath. Dori was back, safe, and now they had to think quickly. "No, but we will be if you don't get into that bathtub, then come down and apologize for sleeping all day."

Dori grimaced. "What, Mom's home?"

"They're *both* here!"

Dori grinned. "You mean Dad made it? That's great! So, what have I been doing, sleeping all day?"

Em waved at the towels on the bed. "That was you."

"Better tell me what else I did."

"You watched adventure movies all last night, you never cleaned your room, you forgot the dishes this morning—I had to dirty two—and oh, you never answered the phone because you took a zillion baths."

Dori snickered, then added, "Oh, I have so much to tell you."

"Tell me later—just go!" Em thrust her sister toward the door.

Dori crept out, peered around, and slipped into the bathroom. Em dug in her drawers and got her some winter clothes, then flung them in after Dori. Then she sagged against the door, this time in real relief.

The girls went down together, Dori with wet hair.

"Hey, Mom," Dori cried, running down to hug her mother. "I'm so glad you're home safe and Gran is better. Hi, Dad! Glad you made it."

Mom hugged her back, and though her mouth was smiling, her eyes frowned a little as Dori flung herself into her dad's arms. "I hope you were more helpful to your sister than it appears," she said.

"Absolutely," Em spoke up quickly. "She made so little mess, it was like she wasn't even here."

Dori stood next to Dad, holding onto his hand. "I promise, Mom, I didn't make one speck of mess for Em to pick up. My room doesn't count, because no one but me has to see it. But now that you are here, I promise I will clean my room until it's as tidy as Em's. How's that?"

Dad was looking from one sister to the other, his eyes a little narrowed.

"All right," Mom said, relenting. "After all, it is vacation. And you two were very good sports about having it ruined by this emergency." She got up. "I had better go over and see how Mrs. Gupta is doing, and thank her for her help." She walked out, grabbing her jacket in the hallway.

Dad sat back. "What's going on, you two?"

Em turned to Dori, feeling sick all over again. Dori looked from her to Dad. "Nothing, Dad," she said.

Dad sighed. "Well, since I don't live here at the moment, it seems unfair to poke my nose into your secrets. As long as they are nothing awful."

Both girls gave sudden, big, delighted smiles.

"Nothing awful at all, Dad," Em said.

"I guess I'll bring my stuff inside—which, incidentally, includes your presents—at least until your mom decides what to do," he said. He put on his coat and went outside.

The girls escaped upstairs, Dori shutting her door and pulling out the medallion.

"I think Dad suspects something," Dori said.

Em sighed. "I wish we could tell him. Do you think we dare?"

Dori rubbed her fingers round and round Ozma's medallion. "Dad has always had an imagination. I think there's a chance that if any grown-up would believe us, it would be Dad."

"Right! So should we tell him? I really, really hated lying."

"I don't blame you. But Em, think about this. If Dad believes us, then either we have a secret with him that Mom doesn't know, or else we have to tell her. Will she believe us?"

"No way." Em shook her head.

Em flopped onto the bed. "I guess we'd better not say

anything. But we're not going to do that ever again."

"I promise," Dori said, raising her hand up.

"Now," Em said. "What is that gold thing around your neck?"

"It's how we'll get back to Oz, but I don't know when, or how we'll manage the time. Though to be strictly fair, I should be the one to have to stay here—"

"No, no, no, no, no," Em said, shaking her head so hard she almost got dizzy. "We both go, or no one goes. Now, tell me about that necklace!"

"I'll tell you everything, but first Ozma said we might be in the middle of a really big adventure of some sort."

"I'm not surprised," Em said. "I saw something in the snow globe. Every time Glinda or Ozma did magic, one of those creepy clouds came, and as soon as they were done, it went away. I wished there was some way to tell them."

Dori made a face. "The necklace will take us to Oz, but I don't think we should use it now. They already know about the clouds, and maybe they know that the clouds come when they do magic."

"Anyway we can't possibly go back to Oz," Em said reluctantly. "Not with Mom just back, and Dad, and us with only a couple days left until school."

The girls looked at each other in silence.

Then Em got the snow globe from where she'd set it on Dori's desk, turning it over and over in her hands. She said, "We'll just keep watch."

Dori nodded. "And maybe we'll find clues. And as for

going back to Oz, there will be a way. If Ozma and Glinda expect us back, that has to mean there will be a way."

"Girls!" a voice came from below. "Nobody wants to cook, and we've all been cooped up by storms too long. Let's go out to dinner!"

"With both Mom and Dad?" Em said to her sister.

Dori whispered, "At least they are being friendly right now. Maybe we'll have fun together, just like when we were little."

Em grinned. "It would be so great to have Mom and Dad be friends again."

Dori tucked the medallion into her top drawer, and Em put the snow globe back onto the desk.

It was time to celebrate the postponed holidays, and to get back to their lives in Kansas. But Oz would never be far from their thoughts.

The prospect of more adventures filled both girls with joy, and they ran downstairs, laughing.

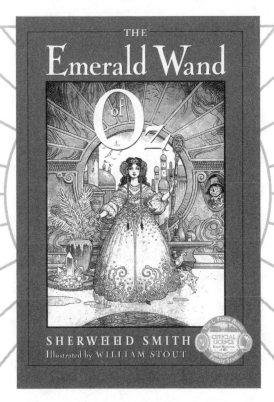